Storlax

To the Atlantic Salmon

First published in 2005
by Meadowside Children's Books
185 Fleet Street, London, EC4A 2HS

Text © Robert Jackson and Bubbi Morthens 2005
Cover illustration by Halldór Baldursson
Endpaper illustration by David Atkinson

A CIP catalogue record for this book is available
from the British Library

Printed in U.A.E

10 9 8 7 6 5 4 3 2 1

Storlax

Robert Jackson • Bubbi Morthens

meadowside
CHILDREN'S BOOKS
Fleet Street, London

Table of Contents

Prologue

Close your eyes and think of the whitest white there ever was; whiter than the whitest cloud and brighter than the brightest star. That's how bright and white it is.

And try, if you dare, to think of a cold so cold that it is colder than the coldest cold from the wintriest of winters; so cold that the sea has turned to ice and snow covers the land.

Now, think of the darkest dark and the blackest black. There has never been a darker black, or a blacker dark, for that is what it is like under the ice-covered sea.

This is where our story begins.

Under the ice in the coldest cold and the blackest black, only the strongest and bravest can survive and so it is that there, with the largest whales, the fiercest sharks, the swiftest seals and the most gigantic of all giant squid, live sleek shoals of... *salmon.*

Think again of the brightest, silvery fish, swimming in the darkest, coldest water there ever was. And try to think of the biggest number you can, more than leaves on a tree, more even than pebbles on a beach, for that's how many salmon there are. See these silver shapes swim and swirl together.

Now, to the sharks, the seals, the whales and the giant squid, all these salmon look the same. But the salmon are able to recognise one another and tell members of the different clans who shoal and swim together.

And finally, picture the bravest strongest salmon, King of the most noble and proudest clan. His name is Storlax. And his family are called the Hofsin.

The Hofsin are one of the hundreds of clans of salmon that winter in the sea of the North. This sea has been their home since anyone can remember. And we are going to learn all about old Storlax, King of the Hofsin, and his noble, brave family, who are preparing to go forth on the Great Journey.

Part 1

The Great Journey

"IT… IS… TIME…!"

The message welled up inside Storlax and then swelled and shuddered from his body, rippling his scales and shaking his gills with great force. A ribbon of lights stretched and moved far and wide across the night sky, shining soft beams of light-power over the snow-covered land and ice-capped seas of the North.

"IT… IS… TIME…!"

On this night only, when the salmon had wintered well and fed their fill, when the scars had healed and their adventures had been told, on this night alone, the Winter Lights penetrated the darkness below. They shone through the blackness, shimmering and glistening on the flanks of the fish as they swam in their shoals.

The message swept through the water like rolling thunder, a shockwave of energy and power. Storlax had received the Power of the Deep and was now transmitting it onwards to his loyal kinsmen.

"IT... IS... TIME...!"

All the Hofsin in the sea were gripped by the message, for them the water ceased to exist, they were floating in Storlax's power.

The shockwaves hammered into the ocean floor, swirling sand in all directions as far as the eye could see. Crabs burrowed deeper into their holes, the razor-toothed conger eel withdrew further into his cave, the giant squid folded his tentacles, and even the killer whale bowed his head in respect. For, of all the fish and mammals in the sea, it was only the salmon who undertook the Great Journey.

Winter was at an end. Spring was on its way. Nothing would ever be the same again.

"Excuse me, where are we going?" a young salmon asked; he seemed unaware that all the other Hofsin had started to swim away, leaving just him and the mighty Storlax to float together.

Storlax remained motionless, ignoring the young salmon who now swam closer to him.

"What is your name?" Storlax asked eventually, his voice a low rumble.

"Salto, Salto of the Hofsin is my name, sir," was the nervous reply.

"… And this is your first time with us on the Great Journey, young Salto of the Hofsin?" Storlax muttered something to himself and then said, "Swim round me boy, tell me what you can see."

Salto was scared and wished that he had stayed with his friend Una and the other young Hofsin.

"Don't worry, my lad, there is nothing to be frightened of!"

Salto swam anxiously around Storlax and saw for the first time the wounds and marks that he had heard so much about. He wanted to flee but knew he had to stay.

"Now, tell me what you see," Storlax encouraged.

Salto looked in wonderment; he knew that many young Hofsin had never been this close to their leader.

He saw three scars, each straight and deep, gouged into Storlax's flesh. He swam to Storlax's head and looked to the noble mouth where he saw a rusted hook imbedded in the corner of his mouth. A few strands of garish colour and a length of twine were still attached. Salto shivered. He could see another smaller hook with sharp pointed barbs imbedded in his leader's cheek. Storlax turned his head to show Salto the eye that had been blinded.

"Have you seen enough, my lad?" Storlax asked.

"Yes, sir, these are the scars of honour that we young Hofsin have been told about…"

Storlax interrupted him. "No, boy. They are scars that I earned from my pride and stupidity. They are the wounds of ignorance. If you ignore what I tell you, you will soon wear them, too, or worse." And then Storlax's voice lightened for the first time. "If I stopped to talk to every young Hofsin we would never get going. I have told you the one thing you need to know and I will say it to you one last time. Every one of these wounds happened when I ignored the Power of the Deep – you must trust it and all it tells you."

Salto thought for a few moments and then, gathering his courage, said, "But I can't feel it, I can't feel the Power of the Deep…"

Storlax sighed, as he had earlier when delivering the message to his clan. Then he swam in a slow circle around Salto, who was bathed in a beam of light that disappeared as quickly as it came.

Salto saw for a flickering instant the place where his life had begun, the Home Pool. He felt its warmth and safety, and his heart swelled with happiness and determination.

"There," said Storlax, "I can do no more. I am weakened enough already. Salto, you have now been touched by the Power of the Deep."

And with a swish of his sturdy tail, Storlax swam away.

The Seals

Una began to wonder where her friend Salto had gone.

She swam the fringes of the shoal to find him. From above, she could see the backs of the Hofsin, purple-black and mottled to protect them from the eyes of the air. From below, she looked upwards and saw, as far as her eye could see, thousands of silvery shapes; silvered to protect them from the eyes of the deep.

She swam away to where the bigger fish were. It was not unusual for Salto to stray but never for this long. For a while, she swam alone in the colder, deeper water.

"Uuuuuna!" It was Salto. She heard his voice and turned happily to greet him.

"What are you doing down here, Una?"

"Where have you been?"

"Oh, nowhere much. I've just been talking to old Storlax and getting the Power of the Deep given to me in person."

"You do talk nonsense, Salto." Una rarely believed the things Salto told her. "Come on, let's join the others. I don't like it down here."

Salto and Una swam away together and joined the shoal of Hofsin. The clan stopped from time to time to eat from the multitudes of capelin and the clouds of krill that they encountered on the way. But mainly they pressed on, swimming with an urgency that neither Salto nor Una had ever known.

The shoal swam into shallower water, where the seabed rose to greet them. The older fish grouped together, working their way along the bed through the rocky crevices that now came into view. Salto looked upwards and saw the underwater explosions caused by diving birds as they plunged into the sea to feed from the smaller fish that swam near the surface.

"Do you know? I was almost hit by one of those things once," Salto said to a Hofsin swimming beside him.

The older fish advised the young Hofsin, "Don't you worry about those. You just eat your fill while you can, my boy. You are going to need all your strength for…"

But he did not finish his sentence. There was a shriek that rent the water. It sounded like the screams of all the lost souls of the Deep escaping at once. The sound came from below and was nearing fast. The Hofsin swam away in all directions in panic and fear. For this was the sound that they feared most, the sound of their most feared predator. It was the sound of seals. Hungry seals.

"Swim deep! They can't reach you down there, swim for your lives!" Storlax's words were just louder than the screeching of the seals. Swim for your lives!" Storlax boomed, as he swam down into the darker, colder water. "Swim deep!"

Una swam as straight as an arrow in pursuit of Storlax and the older Hofsin, but Salto panicked. The dread screeching of seals scorched through his thoughts like a red-hot needle. He tried to listen to Storlax but he couldn't think, he couldn't focus. It was as if he were swimming through clouds of ink. He swam in fear and alarm with some of the younger Hofsin to the shallow water. In the distance he could see rocks and seaweed and hoped that they would bring safety. The seals were close behind.

The chase was on. He turned and swerved, dived and ducked as the shrill screams of the seals grew louder.

They were driving the young Hofsin to the shallower water. The clamour grew and Salto sensed he was in more and more danger. The noise was coming from all sides now; the seals were hounding the salmon, snapping at their tails with their fearsome teeth.

The seals were now swimming amongst the young Hofsin and the noise was unbearable. The screams seared through Salto's mind, his eyes could no longer focus. Then, through the chaos, he could hear Storlax's words: "Swim deep!" At that moment, Salto knew that his only chance of survival was to swim back the way he had come, back through the seals.

Summoning all his courage, he turned to face the seals and the noise that filled him with horror. He swam with all his might, straight into the V-shaped nose, raven-black eyes and whiskery face of a seal, who screeched and squealed as he opened his mouth to devour Salto.

Salto swerved away, his body brushing the seal's skin as he dived downwards and away. He dared not look back. The seal had turned to follow him and Salto twisted and twirled, ignoring the screams, swimming as fast as he could. His life depended on it.

Slowly but surely he swam away from the seal and the noise quietened to a hiss that hummed in his brain.

Through the noise he heard Una's voice: "Salto... Salto... over here!"

Salto looked and saw Una. He swam over to her, his heart beating and the whites of his gills fluttering and trembling.

"Salto! Why didn't you listen to Storlax? Why didn't you follow us?"

Salto was too scared and shocked to reply.

"Oh no," Una said as she stared upwards to the shallows. "Oh no," sadly she repeated the words.

Salto turned and looked to see a red mist hanging in the water. In the midst of the mist, he could for a short time make out the figures of seals chasing salmon and their distant cries.

His eyes were drawn to an object that fell slowly towards him; it floated downwards from side to side... side to side... side to side. His eyes focused in curiosity and then he turned away in horror. It was a body – the bloody body of a young Hofsin.

The Home Scent

Una and Salto watched in silence as the body drifted downwards.

The seals had gone and the sea became quiet again. But it was not as before, for this was a cold quiet. It was the bleakest, saddest silence that the Hofsin can know. It was the first time that Salto and Una had felt this grave quiet – it chilled them to the core.

They watched the body as it rolled over and over, drifting downwards. It descended slowly to the deeper water and on to the mysterious world that lay beyond – the Deep.

"Oh, Una. I was scared… so scared!"

"It's all right, Salto. It's over now. It's all right…" Una tried to calm her friend.

"But that could be me down there. It could be me chopped in half, Una. It could be me on my way to the Deep! I did try to swim down. Honestly, I did. But it all happened so quickly, they were everywhere – there was nowhere to turn."

"Don't worry, Salto. It's finished. Come on, let's join the others. But stay close to me. Please?"

They turned to swim away, but stopped when they saw Storlax emerge from the depths. He was leading a group of young Hofsin. He looked upwards to the bloody water above them.

"Look and learn, everybody – look and learn." His voice was strong, but not at all angry. "This is just the start of our journey and it has not begun well. We have lost friends and family, but that is the way of the Great Journey. Things happen which we cannot control. We can only try our hardest." His voice grew deeper. "The dead have gone to the Deep. They will be happy there. We must not be sad, they would not want us to, but we will remember them."

Storlax's mood lightened. He closed his mouth and drew a deep draught of water through his gills. "Now then, you do the same. What can you smell?" There was excitement in his voice.

Salto looked at Una as she did as Storlax commanded. Slowly, her eyes closed and the corners of her mouth softened and lifted upwards. She could picture a scene from her forgotten childhood. She could taste fresh water. Her gills quivered and soon her fins picked up the rhythm. Her whole body shook.

Salto closed his eyes and breathed as he had seen Storlax do. At first nothing happened and then, slowly, he smelt something new. He saw in his mind the Home Pool and now he could actually smell it. It smelt of peace and safety. It was the Hofsin Home Scent. His body vibrated, sending out waves of ripples to the other Hofsin. He felt newly strong and happy.

One by one, the young Hofsin awoke from their trances and looked warmly at each other. The seals were a distant memory.

"Come on, my brave young Hofsin!" Storlax shouted heartily. "We must all feast. Eat until our stomachs are busting, eat until we can eat no more, until we are fit to burst. It will be our last meal for many a moon!"

The shoals of Hofsin fed happily for several days in the shallow warmer water close to the land. They drifted with the currents, were carried by the tides and each day the scent of the Home Pool grew stronger.

One evening, when the sun set in an explosion of red, orange, purple and gold, and a slither of moon rose and followed the sun's path in the darkening sky to the east, Storlax gathered his clan to tell them it was time to start on the next stage of the Great Journey.

"Hofsin, we are about to leave the sea. You, the older fish, have been here before; for you, the youngsters, this is your first time. For *all* of you I have the same words." Storlax paused and, when he was sure that everyone was listening, he said solemnly, "Follow the Home Scent and trust what your heart tells you is right and it will never let you down. Take your time and travel at your own speed, but always follow the Home Scent. Journey in happiness, for we are honoured to be Hofsin. And, if all goes well, the next time we gather will be beneath the Great Falls. Fare you well, my Hofsin. Fare you well!"

Salto and Una joined a pod of young Hofsin. They swam into the mouth of the estuary, where the water became brackish and they smelt new smells that they had not encountered before. The further they swam into the estuary the fresher the water became. The water became shallower and they swam along the shoreline, using the flooding tides to carry them onwards.

"Do you know that I've just swum past a shoal of sand-eels and I didn't want a morsel? I don't feel hungry at all. Do you think I'm all right, Una?" Salto asked.

Una laughed: "Salto, we were told this would happen. Now, can you smell the Home Pool? It grows stronger every day and it's better than any food."

"Yes, I suppose you're right," Salto replied as they swam on, but he didn't sound convinced.

A little while later, the water grew cloudy and a sickly-sweet smell drifted downstream to greet the Hofsin. Most swam to the centre of the estuary to keep in the clear water, but Salto lagged behind and soon he found himself enveloped in a growing mist. He heard what he thought was a small voice whispering to him.

He stopped and listened hard. There it was again and he could hear what it was saying.

"Come to me. Please come to me." The words were soft and plaintive. "Come to me. Please come to me." He listened hard and heard not one voice, but many small voices all saying the same words: "Come to me. Please come to me."

Salto decided he must ignore the voices, he must follow the Home Scent. He must do as he was told by Storlax. But the misty water blocked out the scent. All he could smell was the sickly sweet odour which was carried down to him on the tide.

"What if these voices need help? Surely it would be right to help those in trouble?" he asked himself. He looked for Una, but she had swum on with the other young Hofsin.

Salto swam into the thickening gloom towards the sound and the voices that grew sweeter and louder.

The Nets of the Dead

"Come to me. Please come to me."

Salto was drawn onwards by the voices. Small pieces of food floated in the mist. He nibbled one piece, cautiously at first, but it tasted so delicious that he ate more. He reached for one particularly appetising piece, but stopped in his wake when he saw a pair of gaunt eyes peering out from behind a net.

Salto could only see the fish's face clearly, the rest of its body was hidden in the mist. Salto thought this was a salmon but wasn't sure. He edged closer. It *was* a salmon but not quite like anything he had seen before.

"Hello, my name's Salto of the Hofsin. Who are you?"

"Hello," the voice replied. "Let me think. I'm not sure that I have a name." The fish ignored a large piece of food that floated down in front of him. "No, it's no good, I don't have a name."

"But you must, everybody has a name. Are you a boy or a girl, then? That'll be a start," Salto asked.

"I'm not sure what you're talking about. I don't know what I am really, other than I'm here and I'm bored with all this food."

"Surely, you can't be fed up?" Salto argued. "It tastes delicious to me."

"I have it all the time. I only eat it out of boredom really."

"Listen, I'm going to have to give you a name if I'm to talk to you. 'Nameless'… that'll do until I think of something better."

"If you like," said Nameless, in a way that sounded as if he were happy to have found a friend.

"So, Nameless, what are doing behind this net? And what's on the other side? Is that where your family are?"

Nameless thought for a while; Salto could see he was concentrating hard: "I can't really answer any of those questions. Oh, wait a second, yes I can. The net goes round in a circle and we live here." He seemed quite pleased with this answer.

Salto was puzzled. "But, what about the Great Journey, the Power of the Deep, the Home Scent? And who is your king? Every clan has a king..."

Nameless looked blankly at Salto. "Sorry, they don't mean a thing to me." He thought some more, "I would like to get out, though. We all would. We feel unwell and we want to get out. That's why we called to you. Will you help us... please?"

"Why, of course I'll help you, Nameless," Salto answered, "but I'm not sure what I can do by myself. I'll go and get Storlax; he'll know what to do."

Salto snapped at a large piece of food and turned to go, "I'll be back as soon as I can."

"You will come back, won't you?" Nameless asked anxiously.

"I promise I will," replied Salto, as he swam away from the net to search for Storlax.

He swam with the tide along the edge of the estuary channel, through a shoal of older fish, to the centre where Storlax presided.

"Storlax," Salto's young voice penetrated the quiet and disturbed his elder's silent progress. "Storlax, please may I speak? I need to talk to you."

"What are you doing, Salto? Why are you disturbing

me and the elders? You should be with the other young Hofsin," said Storlax grumpily.

"I'm sorry to trouble you, but I've found some salmon who are trapped in a net. They need our help to escape. I told them that we would help them. I told them that you would know what to do." Salto hoped that his words would please Storlax.

"I know where you've been, Salto, and there is nothing we can do," Storlax said in a voice that did not invite discussion.

Salto thought of Nameless and the promise that he had made him. "But Storlax, I told him I would come back and help them. I told them that you, our King, would know what to do… I promised them."

Salto heard the voices of the elders muttering, "Well, really!" and calling him "Wretched boy!"

"Salto, there is nothing we can do, we must swim on. We have troubles of our own to worry about. Our way ahead is perilous enough as it is."

"But, I promised, Storlax, I gave my word…" Salto felt the anger of the elders and the disapproval of Storlax and was about to swim away when he heard the voice of his king.

"We'll go, Salto. Follow me," he said gravely.

Storlax and Salto swam in silence against the tide, the younger fish struggling to keep up. In a while, they arrived to where the water became cloudy.

"Come to me. Please come to me," they could hear the voices plead as they swam slowly onwards, until they reached the net.

"This is a terrible place, Salto. We call it the Nets of the Dead. It is a place full of sadness and sorrow. Can you hear those voices? They all sound the same. And can you smell that sickly sweet smell?"

"Nameless will be here somewhere, I know he will." Salto called out, "Nameless! Nameless!"

Storlax shook his head sadly. "He'll have forgotten, Salto. It's the way it is with these fish that are put here by the Shadows. There is nothing we can do. Salto, I'm sorry. You have fulfilled your promise, you have returned, but there is nothing to be done."

"But we must. These are salmon!" Salto begged.

"Salto, you must listen to me. These fish live here for a while, are fattened up and then disappear. It is the same every year. These are dark, hopeless places," Storlax said and tried to make the young Hofsin understand.

He turned onto his side and with his mighty tail fanned clear water into the cage. It cleared a space in the soupy water in which there circled thousands of fish, who all looked exactly the same as Nameless. They swam trance-like around the edge of the netting, their mouths opening and closing as they ate the food that fell from above.

"Look closely, Salto!"

Salto looked at the fish and saw that their tails were small and frayed and that their fins were tattered and lay flat against their bodies. He saw that their shoulders were fat and humped forward towards their heads, which were small and measly looking. Their eyes were empty, hollow and helpless. It was the saddest sight Salto had ever seen.

Storlax himself was distressed. "Yes, these are salmon, but they are not like us. They are not clan salmon. It is terrible what happens here. These fish still have their wild instincts; they still long to leap the great falls; they ache to swim the wide oceans and enjoy the companionship of the shoal. But they can't and this is why they are such sad and sorry fish. They have no adventures, no happiness, just sickly food and a trance-like swim around the rim of the net... now follow me!"

Salto followed as they swam down to the bottom of the netting and again Storlax pushed clear water into the cage so that they could see. The sight that greeted them made Salto whimper. Scattered across the base netting, fish lay dead and dying, their skin white and peeling; some twitching in the silty mist, some lying deathly quiet. Storlax motioned for Salto to follow him, as he swam downwards to the seabed. The water here was even thicker and again Storlax fanned in clean water with his tail. Where rocks and weed used to be, there was only a thick blanket of creamy silt. As far as the eye could see, food and waste from the net drifted down onto the ocean floor, which blistered and boiled slow bubbles of noxious gas. Salto watched sadly as a crab shell drifted across in the current like a slowly rolling tumbleweed in a desert of starfish.

"We have seen enough. Come on, Salto, we must press on, we must join our Hofsin."

Storlax and Salto swam away from the Nets of the Dead in silence.

Red Belly

Salto swam beside Storlax away from the Nets of the Dead. There was so much he wanted to ask, so much he needed to know, but he was too shocked to speak. He looked at the scars on Storlax's flank and realised for the first time that these had been caused by seals. He thought of his own fear and the pain that Storlax must have endured; he thought of Nameless in the nets. Life seemed so bleak. He swam even closer to his King, so close that their flanks touched from time to time as they swam to rejoin their clan.

"Salto, you have seen the Nets of the Dead, you swam under them, a place where few ever go. What you have seen will never leave you but, take heart, it is another world. It is the world of the Shadows, not our world."

"Who are the Shadows?" asked Salto.

"We salmon know only one thing about the Shadows and that is that they cannot be trusted. All who live in the oceans accept that we are part of a great chain – small fish are eaten by those bigger than they. We salmon eat fish, bigger seals and sharks eat us and, when we die, our souls go to the Deep, our bodies sink to the deepest deep to feed the smallest fish and so it all begins again. That's the way it is. But the Shadows are not part of the Deep. They only take."

Salto tried to picture all the different fish in the sea joined together by the Deep, but it was too much for his young mind. He could only ask, "How do you know all this?"

"I know this, Salto, because it is the truth. Every year on the third moon of our journey, I swim to Raven's Pool to attend the Parliament of the Animals. On that night, all animals – Fin, Fur and Feather – gather and speak with one tongue. Eagle is their king and, for that night alone, all are at peace with one another. That is how we fish learn what is going on in the world above, and how we tell the Fur and the Feather what is happening in the oceans."

He paused to look at Salto, who was spellbound in his gaze, and Storlax remembered for a while what it had been like when he was a first-run salmon.

"There is much sadness and danger in our lives, Salto; the Great Journey used to be such a happy time. Yes, there were challenges, but they were the challenges we were destined to meet. Now there is danger everywhere. The Shadows plunder the seas, taking every living creature they can find. They lay traps for us on the Great Journey and they make our rivers and nurseries sick. They rear those diseased, nameless fish to eat. We have much to fear from them and we are powerless to change anything. Our only hope is to believe that the Power of the Deep will prove stronger than their evil."

He looked Salto in the eye: "I sense there may be great things ahead for you, my young Hofsin, but you must not rush in so easily." Storlax's voice regained its regal composure. "Think and trust or it will all come to nothing – think and trust. Now, I must join the elders and tell them about what we have seen." And with one sweep of his mighty tail he was gone.

Salto swam away from Storlax. At first he felt comforted by being with his King, but then he remembered the Nets of the Dead and tried to imagine the Shadows who kept salmon caged. He began to doubt whether he was capable of making the Great Journey. He wanted to speak to Una; she always helped at times like these.

Salto swam the shoals of Hofsin trying to find her, but she was nowhere to be found. He wanted to talk to the other Hofsin but they ignored him. Instead they stayed in their groups, following the elders.

Salto swam into the fringe of the estuary to rest in the slack water. He lay still for a while, fighting away sadness and wondering what to do next. It all seemed so pointless. He was lonely, tired and, more than anything else, miserable.

He sighed and then, although he tried not to, he sobbed and cried until his eyes were dry.

"Now then, what's the matter with you?" a voice came from the strangest fish that Salto had ever seen. "We can't have you pouring your salt out here, young man. That'll never do. Now, what's your problem?"

"I don't think you'd understand my problem," said Salto forlornly, as he looked at the fish more closely. He had a face that looked as if it had been slapped by a whale's tail. But, somewhere behind the ridges and wrinkles, Salto could make out what seemed to be a permanent smile. "Thank you, anyway," Salto added.

"In case you're wondering, my name is Red Belly and you are welcome to what I like to call my home. I don't have many visitors, so I'm afraid I can't offer you much." Red Belly scrumpled up his face even more. "Now, let me guess. Who are you? Don't tell me! Let me work it out..." Red Belly moved surprisingly quickly for his size, and in no time at all he had swum around, under and over Salto.

"I know who you are! You came by this way with a crowd of noisy smolts. Last year it was. My word, you've filled out into a fine young salmon. The feeding grounds have treated you well, I see."

Salto thought for a while. He had been told that all the young Hofsin had started life in the river but he could not remember ever being there. "Are you sure it was me, Red Belly?"

"I'm sure, I'm sure. You rascals nearly pushed me off my rock. You're one of Storlax's tribe. I'd recognise the sleek lines and the aristocratic chin anywhere! You are the spitting image of the old boy himself when he was your age."

"Do you *know* Storlax?" Salto was impressed.

"Well, we're not that well acquainted, but I've seen him coming and going for many years now. He's a fine fellow and no mistake. We all know about him." Red Belly belched before continuing, "He keeps his standards, that's what I like about him."

Salto had stopped crying, leaving streaks of salt across his cheeks, but he was unsure of whether he could trust Red Belly. He looked cautiously at him.

"So what are you upset about? You can tell me." Red Belly scrunched another smile at Salto.

"I just feel that I can't do it – the Great Journey, the Power of the Deep – it's all so confusing. Everyone else seems to find it so much easier than me. I keep making mistakes and getting into trouble, and nobody understands that I'm scared and confused."

Red Belly started to laugh, and he laughed until the wrinkles on his face wobbled in all directions. "*You're* sad and lonely? What about *me*? I'm here on my own, because nobody wants to be with me. I'm so ugly that when I swim past the mussels hide in their shells. I'm so hideous that the crabs bury themselves in the sand, the octopuses shoot ink at me and the seals pretend to be on a diet! That's sad and lonely, my lad. But, you know what? I'm the happiest fish in the neighbourhood. You ask anyone."

"How can you be?" asked Salto grumpily.

"Every morning when I wake up I tell myself it's going to be a good day. And do you know what? If I say that, it almost always is. Now, you pull yourself together, get a grip and cheer up. The best thing you can do is set off to join your family and elders. And I'll give you one piece of advice..." Red Belly belched again, "... take it from me, listen to the elders; they know more than you think, and they've seen it all before. If you're ever feeling sad again just think of old Red Belly lying on his rock watching the world go by. He knows you've got nothing to worry about."

Salto felt happier as he watched Red Belly swim backwards towards him to slap tails in friendship and farewell. Their tails swiped against each other and then Red Belly added:

"One last thing, young Hofsin. I have a little trick I do whenever I feel upset. I breathe in..." Red Belly opened his gaping rubbery mouth and his body filled like a great shiny ball, "... and then I blow it out the other end!" There was a huge explosion of bubbles and Red Belly was propelled past Salto like a balloon with a hole in it.

"Goodbye, young Hofsin, come and see me again soon!" Red Belly's voice was lost as he was blown away into the distance.

The Seagulls

Salto swam away from Red Belly and was happy once more. He could smell the Home Scent and propelled himself eagerly towards it. As he swam along he noticed that the water was becoming less salty and it was not long before he saw a large group of Hofsin, gathered in a deep hollow. He also saw Una, who had been looking anxiously for him. She swam upwards to greet him.

"I've been looking for you. Are you all right?"

"I'm fine. I've made a new friend and I've learnt the most amazing trick, you wait until I show it to you." Salto started to suck in, as he had seen Red Belly do, but then became embarrassed in front of Una and decided not to. "I may need a bit of practice first," he said. "What are all these fish doing here, why have we stopped?"

"We are about to enter the river. This water is really strange. None of us really like it yet. From time to time groups set off upstream and they wallow around for a while and then return. I haven't a clue how we are all meant to get up there."

Salto asked, "How far have you gone?"

"Not very far, it's very shallow and bright, and all the fish, even the elders, are jittery."

"Come on, Una, let's give it a try, I'm sure it's what we're meant to do."

"I'm not so sure, Salto. Why don't we wait until one of the elders takes a group?"

"Come on, follow the Home Scent. That's what Storlax said, don't you remember?" He sniffed audibly. "And there, can't you smell it? I'll go and gather a few of the other young Hofsin and we can set off together. Safety in numbers, safety in numbers," Salto said in a voice that sounded like one of the elders.

Soon they had gathered a group of fish and they set off from the hollow. Salto led with Una swimming closely beside him.

"Keep an eye out for seals, everybody, we know what harm they can do," Una said as they swam over a sandbar and into the main current of fresh water. The water stung their eyes at first and made them feel queasy, but they swam on, pushing hard against the current and ignoring their discomfort. Salto felt proud to be at the head of the group with Una by his side.

The water became shallow again, the seabed shelving upwards into the distance.

"I think we've gone far enough for this trip. We can come back again tomorrow," said Una.

"Just a little bit further, we are doing so well…" Salto turned to urge the rest of the party on and was sad to see that many had already turned to go back out to the estuary. "Spoilsports!" he shouted at them as he turned to Una. He saw, on the surface behind her, many bouncing shapes that grew larger and darker. "Watch out, Una! Look out behind you!"

The shapes moved quickly and became small explosions in the water around Una. Salto could make out the claws of the gulls sweeping past Una's head, many of them diving and driving the Hofsin on to the sandbank. Una was surrounded by the birds, who splashed and dived all around her. She tried to swim to the deeper water, but each time she tried to escape, a gull blocked her way.

"Swim to me, Una, swim to me!" Salto looked on, helpless, as one of the gulls attached himself to Una's back in the shallow water. It flapped its wings frantically to lift her body so that it was easier to drag up the sandbank. It was trying to peck out her eyes. Una writhed and splashed and fought the gull away as bravely as she could but the gull had her tightly in its grasp. Salto's alarm turned to anger. He summoned all of his courage and swam into the shallow water, where sand and pebbles grazed his belly. He charged with all his might and managed to ram her from off the bottom, where she had begun to flounder. The blow winded Una but also unbalanced the gull, who flew away in squawking frustration. Salto and Una found themselves slithering into a shallow gully, which drained back into the sea. Here they were able to swim and writhe their way back to deeper water. The gulls threw themselves recklessly at the two young Hofsin and pecked and clawed at their heads and backs as Salto and Una squirmed, wriggled and fought their way to freedom.

Una and Salto looked back helplessly as they saw another Hofsin driven up the bank and then lost sight of him altogether, as his body became shrouded in spray, beaks and claws.

"Salto, this is horrible! Those poor fish, our friends…" Una panted, her gills pumping water and air into her gasping lungs. Salto looked at her back, and was relieved to see that her scratches, whilst bloody, were not deep. His relief also eased the guilt he was feeling for leading the young Hofsin astray. He was about to say something when Una said sharply, "Salto, we shouldn't have left the others, we shouldn't have followed you!" and then added, "Come on, let's gather the others and go back to the elders. We must tell what has happened." She swam away, leaving Salto to follow her.

Salto swam to catch up with her. "It wasn't my fault… it wasn't my fault…" he said, and then added sheepishly, "I really didn't mean this to happen… I didn't know."

But Una was too shocked by the attack and too annoyed with Salto to reply.

Word soon spread through the Hofsin about the seagull attack. The shoals huddled more tightly together in the estuary, wanting neither to go backwards nor forwards. They were an unhappy clan that evening, as the moon rose and hovered coldly in the pale night sky. Storlax knew that at daybreak this moon would bring the highest tide for some time, and the best chance that the bigger fish would have to cross the sandbar into the river.

He called the elders to him. "So, we are nearing the Shadowgate. The tide will not let us pass under it at night and there are gulls everywhere who have already feasted on Hofsin. I will not risk losing any more this way. Our only choice is to wait until the dawn and let the tide carry us into the river. But this will mean that we will enter the river in daylight, there will be Shadows everywhere, and we will have to be vigilant."

The elders knew that Storlax was right and, while none felt easy at the prospect of travelling during the day, they all agreed it was the best thing to do. They trusted their King.

And so, throughout the night, Storlax watched as the elders mustered their shoals and waited with them for dawn and high tide. Soon the first rays of dawn brightened the surface of the water and their bodies felt the gentle surges of the flooding tide. It was time to enter the river.

"Swim fast and deep as you can, my Hofsin, fast and deep. The Home Pool is calling us home! We are nearly at the Shadowgate. Ahead lie the safe pools at the bottom of the river; we will soon be able to rest and adjust."

Storlax swam gingerly across the bar and into the mouth of the river and soon felt at ease. He swam gladly, safe in the knowledge that the estuary and its dangers were behind them. Salto travelled beside him, elated as his head filled with the strong scent of the Home Pool. They were now swimming in pure fresh water, the stinging in his eyes had gone and all thoughts of food had disappeared.

As the morning wore on, the sun rose in the sky and soon was shining directly downstream into the eyes of the advancing Hofsin. The clear water provided no cover from its glare. They swam as fast as they could, only resting where they could find shade behind a boulder or beside a bank.

Storlax and Salto rounded a sheltered bend in the river and ran into a shoal of Hofsin who were swirling restlessly in circles. Ahead of them, the brilliant brightness of the sun was half eclipsed by a dark, black slab of dead light. It hovered menacingly above the surface, spilling its shade like a pool of oil outwards towards them, a glowering, sinister barrage blocking their way upstream. None were brave enough to swim onwards and into it.

Storlax swam forward. "This is the Shadowgate. It's the place where the Shadows cross the river, but you mustn't fear it, my Hofsin. We need to be careful, but we're safe under its shade."

As he said this, a huge rumbling, rattling tremor sent sound and shockwaves through the water. A large dark shape flashed across the sun from one side of the Shadowgate to the other. It went as quickly and as noisily as it had come. The Hofsin around Storlax swam ever more nervously. Some even started to head backwards downstream.

"Follow me. Don't be afraid, my Hofsin. We mustn't lose heart. We are safe in the shade of the Shadowgate. But we must go carefully." Storlax's voice was measured but showed his concern. He led the way forward and soon felt Salto nudging along beside him. "Well done lad, well done." As he spoke, another dark shape grew out of the Shadowgate's shade, stretching ominously out to meet them. "Stop. Don't move!" whispered Storlax, as it lengthened towards them. "A Shadow."

Salto resisted the temptation to turn and swim away as Storlax warned, "Your first Shadow, Salto. You have been told much about them, and now you see one. Promise me, always be careful when you see their shade… always be careful, my boy. Pretend that you are as lifeless as a rock." Salto did as he was told and made only the smallest movements of his tail to keep still against the current.

Beside him, Storlax lay motionless in the Shadow's outline, which swelled unevenly across the riverbed. He felt as anxious as he had all those years ago on his first Great Journey. His anxiety grew, for Storlax knew that the journey had not started well; the seals, the Nets of the Dead and now the seagulls had made his Hofsin nervous and fearful. He knew, better than any, what perils lay awaiting them on the other side of the Shadowgate. "Perhaps this Shadow leaning over to meet them was a bad omen," he thought. And then an even darker notion crept into Storlax's mind: "Perhaps this journey was doomed from the start."

As he lay a few yards downstream of the Shadowgate, Storlax could feel the Shadow's eyes scouring the water around him. Also he could feel, for the first time in a long while, the hook lodged in the corner of his mouth and, with that feeling, came the memory of the fear in his heart during his last escape from the Shadows. Storlax felt his resolve weaken. He thought of the Hofsin who had been with him on the last Great Journey, he thought of those who had failed to return to the sea, and he wondered how many would survive this journey upstream to the Home

Pool. All the while, the Shadow gazed onto and through the water, down to the river bed itself, its eyes searching for the slightest movement or flash of silver that would betray where Storlax and Salto lay.

"It will begin soon..." Storlax murmured. "It will begin soon." He sighed as he willed himself to overcome his fear and lead his Hofsin onward, beyond the Shadowgate.

part 2

The Long Shadow

And still the Shadow stood gazing into the river.

Below, Storlax lay silently, willing himself to forget his fear and to ignore the doubt that had taken hold in his mind. He lifted his head a fraction and opened his mouth to let the river water wash through his gills. He could taste the Home Scent and he sensed the soft buffeting of the current along the full length of his body; it was like a balm. His eyes deadened, shutting out all light, and his heartbeat eased to a slow and regular 'bump'. He became unaware of time and heedless of the Hofsin around him. In his mind, Storlax could picture a borderless darkness, he could hear only the soft beat of his heart as his body swayed lightly in the river's flow. The King surrendered himself to the river.

He lay like this for a while until he could picture the river at a time before the Shadows had arrived. He could see the way ahead as it was all those years ago without the Shadowgate. Then images appeared of all the Storlax who had led their Hofsin before him into the river. These noble ancestors spoke with one voice, "Storlax of the Hofsin, this is your river! This is your destiny!" These words filled him with courage.

Storlax emerged slowly from his trance and could feel once again the Shadow's eyes seeking him out, raking the river bed for Hofsin. A deep pride welled up inside the King. He left the safety of the river bed and drifted to the surface of the river. He allowed his body to float so that his back was out of the water. There, visible to the world above, were the scars of his journeys and there, too, the hooks and barbs left from his struggles with the Shadows. Fearlessly, he swam forwards until he was directly under the Shadow. There he remained, defiant in front of the dark sinister form, as if to say, "I AM STORLAX, KING OF THE HOFSIN. HOW DARE YOU LOOK DOWN ON ME!" His defiance was more eloquent than words could ever be.

Storlax held himself in this position for some time and then turned in the water and swam back, down to where Salto lay watching in awe. "Come forward with me, my boy, we will rest under the Shadowgate until we are ready to go further."

Una witnessed Storlax defy the Shadow and, while it had given the other Hofsin new heart, it only made her more aware of the dangers ahead. She was taking longer to adapt to the fresh water; she still felt queasy, and her eyes still smarted. Swimming in the river's shallow clear water under the sun's bright light made her feel hunted and vulnerable. The wounds that she had received from the gull stung and she couldn't stop thinking about the other Hofsin, beached and helpless, ravaged by the gulls. In dread of the Shadows, she felt hopelessly inadequate to face the river and its challenges. Despite all these fears Una swam forwards into the shade below the Shadowgate, hoping that these feelings would go away.

The tide rose again and brought with it a small shoal of salmon from the Straxin clan, who made much noise and commotion as they came to rest under the Shadowgate. Storlax had earlier warned his young Hofsin: "Leave those skinny racers well alone, let them get on with it. 'More haste, less speed' is our motto. Don't let these tearaways lead you astray."

The Straxin and the Hofsin – both had to use the same estuary and river mouth to enter their home river. Their junction was a short distance beyond the Shadowgate. There had always been, for as long as anyone could remember, rivalry between the clans and squabbles often broke out.

"Hello, my beauty!" a fine young Straxin said to Una as he splashed into the lie. "Do you mind if I join you while I get my breath back?"

"Of course not. It's good to have new company," she replied, looking over at Salto who ignored her completely. "How far have you come today?"

"We've come from the sea, into the estuary and up to the Shadowgate, all in one day. Pretty good going, I'd say. We don't hang around waiting for our elders all the time like you Hofsin."

"But isn't it dangerous?"

"No way, that's just Hofsin talk. The quickest way's the best way. And when *we* move, we *really* move. It's all about getting there for us. It's much more fun that way. Try it. Call me Drax, by the way," he added with a twinkle in his eye. "You can come along with us if you like."

"I'm not sure that I should," said Una, although she longed to get away from the Shadowgate. She also noticed that Drax was a fine-looking salmon. "I'm not sure it's wise," she added.

"Thought so, just another stuffy Hofsin. You're all the same, you lot." Drax saw the other Straxin swim away. "Look, the others are heading off, I'd better go with them. This place gives me the creeps. All I can tell you is that we'll be in the safest, darkest pool known to salmon by nightfall, and not a Shadow in sight. Come along! You can always swim back to this lot if you don't like it."

"I'm not sure."

"I thought you said you didn't like it here and I don't blame you. This place isn't called 'Shadowgate' for nothing."

"I don't, but I should stay with my family."

"Well, take it or leave it. I don't mind, I've got to get going." As Drax said this, the whole river around the Shadowgate rumbled and vibrated once more, sending shockwaves through the water, and just as it had done earlier, a huge shade swept across the water below them. The thunderous noise and vibration shook Una to the core; she was terrified. She took one last look over at Salto and then, without saying a word, set off behind the fast-swimming Straxin.

Drax was true to his word. They swam fast and straight, not stopping or resting, nor taking time to talk. From time to time Una dropped back and Drax swam behind her and pushed her forward with his nose. The excitement that she felt when they set off from the Shadowgate was replaced by a growing weariness. She also became anxious. The scent of the Home Pool had disappeared completely and the water became murky with strange, unwelcoming scents.

"Come on, don't dawdle! We've got to get past this place where the Shadows live. If we stop here we'll never get going again," Drax shouted to Una as he edged away from her.

"But I need to rest, I must rest…" said Una.

"Are you mad? Can't you taste the water? The Shadows have killed the river here. We must swim upstream," Drax replied as he swam onwards.

Una swam as fast as she was able against the strong current that pushed out to the sides of the river, but couldn't keep up with the Straxin. She carried on for as long as she could, but the gap between them grew and grew.

"Why can't you wait for me? Please wait for me!" Una pleaded, as Drax disappeared around a bend in the river.

He never looked back. She swam under the riverbank in despair.

For the first time in her life, Una was alone.

The Straxin River

A shoal of smolts had bundled and tumbled into the Shadowgate pool and were causing havoc amongst the Hofsin. They darted from one side of the pool to the other, chasing each other in all directions. The pool filled with the sound of their merry laughter. Finally they formed into a long line and, like the largest eel in the sea, they each followed the one in front as they wound their way around the length and breadth of the pool.

"Oops, sorry!" said one smolt, as he crashed into Storlax.

"Smolts," muttered Storlax grumpily. "I had hoped for some peace and quiet but it seems our younger brethren have other plans." He sank to the shade of a large boulder to seek quiet, but in truth was happy to see their healthy faces and hear their cheerful laughter.

"You had all better calm down a bit. That was Storlax you just bumped into," said Salto.

"Why are you all so glum? We're on our way down to the sea, we're leaving the river and, all together now…" the smolts shouted in unison, "WE ARE HAPPY!"

Storlax let out another mighty groan.

The snake of smolts darted across the pool but the smallest smolt peeled off from the tail of the line to talk to Salto.

"Hello, my name is Brynjar. All you big fish, are you travelling together?"

"Yes, we are on our way upstream on the Great Journey. We've come a long way these last few moons. We've swum from the sea where you are now headed. There you will feed and grow into fine young Hofsin," replied Salto, who looked kindly on these young fish. "You had better swim off and join the others, they will soon be on their way."

"Can't I come with you? I'm not sure that I want to leave the river."

"No, you must go. You have happy times ahead of you," Salto advised.

"But is it safe out there? I'm the smallest of them all."

"You'll be fine, Brynjar. Keep a look out and keep together. That's all that you have to remember."

"Come on, Shrimp! It's time to go!" shouted the leader of the line.

Brynjar looked doubtfully at Salto, who smiled and said, "We'll soon be on our way too, the elders are getting restless. Go on, get going, you can't always be the last in line."

And, with those words, he shooed Brynjar away and went to join the shoal leaving the Shadowgate.

———

The bank where Una lay had eroded away in the winter floods, leaving a fence pole and a tangle of barbed wire to dangle in the water. A large sheet of plastic had wrapped itself around the wire and the post. In the slack water above this man-made barrier, rubbish thrown into the river had collected and a slimy scum formed on the surface. Una was sheltered by a canopy of polystyrene cups and plastic bottles, which stuck to the surface in a pool of oil from a car engine that had been dumped in the river. She lay under this filth, too tired to find another place. Shadows moved along the bank and there were sounds and noises that she had never heard before.

Una could feel the footsteps of a Shadow walking towards her, its vibrations pulsing from the bank. She could not swim away because her route was blocked by the wire and plastic, and she was too frightened to swim back towards the Shadow. She was trapped. The vibrations grew stronger and she panicked, turned and tried to wriggle her way through the wire and plastic. She forced her body through a hole, and pushed and pushed and squirmed as hard as she could. She could see clear water ahead. She was nearly through when the pole fell further into the water, covering her tail in plastic. She was stuck. The more she wriggled the more stuck she became. Worse still, oil dripped down to the water around her and she was soon floating in a putrid soup, gasping for her life.

She fought to free herself and, as she twisted and turned, a dark silver shape was freed from below and floated up towards her. At first she was curious but then she gasped with horror, for there, looking blankly back at her, were the eyeless sockets of a dead salmon, its flesh hanging in shreds from its bones. Riding on its back was a sewer rat, tearing at what remained of the rotting tissue.

She tried to find words but none came. She wanted to cry out but she couldn't. Una tried not to suck in the water but she could feel the slime in her gills choking the life from her body. She sent out messages of alarm but she knew it was hopeless.

Una heard a voice muttering and humming to itself. It sounded like an elder, but his voice was somehow strange.

"Gone the wrong way, must go back, time to turn back, Rocky," said the voice again in its gentle monotone.

She struggled more as the rat swam away from the carcass, brushing along her body on its way to the surface and air. It wouldn't be long until he returned to feast on her.

"Help! Help me!" pleaded Una. "Somebody please help me. I'm over here!"

Una heard the voice reply in questions to itself. "Whoa… hold on. Whoa… who's that…? Sounds like a Hofsin…"

"Help me! Please, help me. I'm over here." Una gurgled roughly, the oily water working its way deeper into her throat. She strained to see where the voice was coming from and slowly the shape of a giant salmon emerged from the murky darkness. He had a noble head with a kindly face that had a short scar over one eye.

"Hofsin, a pretty young Hofsin, now what are you doing here? We'd better get you out." His head moved in small, slow jerks as he spoke, the eye below the damaged forehead seemed to focus more lazily than the other. "And you don't look too well sir, I must say," he said to the decomposing fish, which was now floating beside Una in the mire. "Is he your friend?" Una's rescuer asked lightly.

"No, he's not! Get the beastly thing away from me, please. And please, help me get out of here, I can hardly breathe."

"Yes, yes. This river is dying. We must get you out, what is your name?" The fish seemed completely unaffected by the pollution and Una's plight.

"Una," came the gasped reply.

"Well, mine's Rocky," he said as if they were enjoying a gentle paddle in safe waters.

Rocky swam closer to Una and looked at her tail and saw that the plastic had wrapped tightly around her. He mumbled to himself as he tried to work out what to do. There was a loose flap but a strand of barbed wire hung menacingly close.

"Mmhh… there's not much I can do to help," said Rocky. " Una, you are well and truly stuck."

"I know that! You must be able to do something. Please do something?" choked Una.

"I said that there wasn't much that *I* can do to help you. Now listen to me and do as I tell you." He paused for a while and then said in a deeper voice, "Darken your mind…"

" I need help, not a rest…" coughed Una.

"Please, it will help," coaxed Rocky. "Now, darken your mind and think of your Hofsin Home Scent. Try, please?"

At first Una could only smell the oil and the Shadows – she had been too long away from her river – but then a faint scent appeared and grew slowly. She had found remnants of her Home Scent in her mind and willed herself to focus on it. Rocky could see her body relax.

"Now think of the Power of the Deep welcoming you home, see it in your mind," his voice was still a quiet monotone.

Una saw soft pulsating tendrils of light. They combined with her Home Scent to fill her senses. Together they took away all her fear and made her calm. Her body became limp, her gills barely opening. She lay like this for a short while.

"And now," whispered Rocky, "push forward with your fins and swim down to me."

Una lifted from her trance and did as she was told. Her limp tail slipped easily from its restraints, and with her fins she inched herself down and away from the watery dungeon. She drifted down to the river bed where Rocky waited.

He smiled warmly at her. "There you are, you didn't need me after all."

"Thank you," she croaked weakly.

"We had better get going. They'll be missing you," Rocky said as he nudged Una into the current. She was too exhausted to reply but in her heart she knew she had learnt much from this kindly giant of a fish. She had overcome her fear of the river. Una was newly strong as the downstream current pushed against her tail and carried her back to the junction with her home river.

Rocky

Rocky picked a route that ran in the slacker water beside the banks. From time to time they would turn upstream in the eddy behind a boulder to rest and catch their breath. At these times Una would try to talk to Rocky. There was so much that Una wanted to ask him but he seemed happier in his own world, the world where he mumbled and chattered to himself. He was the biggest salmon she had ever seen, bigger than Storlax and the other elders, but he wasn't a Hofsin. There was something almost childlike about him.

Soon the cleaner water washed the worst of the pollution from their gills. The foul stench of the Shadow's home was behind them as they made their way back to the junction. When they turned the corner to head upstream into the Hofsin river, the scent of the Home Pool was present in every drop of water.

"Can you smell that, Rocky? Isn't it welcoming?" she asked, as she swam to the strongest part of the current, to luxuriate in the fragrance and let the river wash away the last remnants of the Shadows.

"Smells and scents. You Hofsin like your homey smells. They're all the same to Rocky."

They swam onwards to the Tern Pool and soon found Storlax's shoal of Hofsin, where an elder swam to greet them.

Rocky saw her and slipped out of view, leaving Una to confront the elder alone.

"Una, where have you been? Storlax wants to see you. And he's not happy."

Una followed the elder to the deepest part of the pool where Storlax rested with his tail towards them. She could see his mighty frame and his fins were shaking in a way that they had not seen before. She waited for him to speak.

Storlax turned slowly to her, his face filled with anger.

"I will not ask you to say that you are sorry. What you have done is far too serious for any apology. Una, you left the safety of your home river, the Home Scent and your family to go on a jaunt with the Straxin. It was wrong. It is as simple as that – it was wrong!"

Una wanted to try to explain why she had swam away from the Shadowgate, but she felt helpless in front of Storlax, who shuddered with rage. Una quaked in front of him but in the background she could hear Rocky's voice saying:

"Oh, bubble, bubble…"

Storlax could not hear him, and continued to Una, "I'm angry, but not at you. I am angry at myself for not making sure you had learnt these simple lessons…"

Rocky drew closer and repeated, "Oh, bubble, bubble. Storlax, you don't change. Bubble, bubble…"

"Rocky?" Storlax's mood lightened immediately. "I'd know that voice anywhere. Come out where I can see you, my old friend."

"Bubble, bubble. Don't you be too hard on young Una – she has been brave." Rocky's voice had found a strength that Una had not heard earlier. She had never heard anyone talk to Storlax like this before and although she was happy to have his support, she was also scared that Rocky's intervention would only make the King even more angry.

"I am sorry, Storlax, even if it is not enough to say it. I am sorry for letting you and the Hofsin down," she said earnestly.

"We are just glad that you are back safe and sound," Storlax replied. His dark mood had gone. There was a new sparkle in his eye. "Now, you go and get the other young Hofsin. I have something important to show you all."

Una swam away to gather the other young Hofsin. She wanted to find Salto and tell him of her rescue by Rocky.

"And as for you Rocky, we have much to talk about. Will you travel the Great Journey by my side? Can I persuade you to take on the Great Falls one more time?"

Rocky twitched his head and slowly rolled his eye. "So long as I don't have to hear 'bubble bubble' all the time." And then, with an earnest look, he added, "Of course I'll journey with you, Storlax."

"Well, that's agreed then. Forgive me for a moment as I must prepare myself for the youngsters." And with these words Storlax swam in a stately circle around the pool.

Una assembled the other young Hofsin. They looked on curiously as Storlax swam around them. They could see the scars and the hooks, distinct against the purples and blacks of his back. The shimmering silver of his belly seemed brighter in the river's fresh water.

"Now, watch me," Storlax commanded as he completed his circle. He turned to look at them and then swam away down to the depths of the pool. He swerved upwards and, with several hard beats of his tail, propelled himself to the surface. As he shot through the water he let out a happy cry of "Aaah…!" that grew louder as he neared the surface. Just when the young Hofsin thought that he would turn away, he thrashed his mighty tail even harder and, with one final twist of his body, broke through the surface. He disappeared in a swirl of ripples and splashes. He was gone.

For what seemed like seconds, the young Hofsin looked on in wonder, some in distress. But as quickly as he had vanished, Storlax's enormous frame plunged back into the water. His cry of "Aaaaaaaah…!" was now laced with laughter and elation.

"There is nothing, absolutely nothing, that we Hofsin like more than a good leap into the warm air!" he laughed. "Look again, my young friends; it will soon be your turn."

Storlax showed the young salmon how to leap. First he demonstrated the basic 'up, out and belly-flop'. Then there was the graceful 'rainbow leap', which saw him porpoise through the surface and return several feet away, hardly making a splash as he returned to the water. He then showed them the 'tail-walk', teaching them how to walk on their tails across the surface of the water. Finally, he taught them the best trick of all, the 'leap, twist and sideways splash', which made the biggest commotion above and under the water.

"Now it's your turn, my young Hofsin. Leap and play to your hearts' content. Swim and jump until you are weary."

Salto had watched Storlax's display with eager excitement and could not wait to start. He swam downwards as he had seen Storlax do and then beat his tail with all his might. He could feel the water rush past his face and the slippery tickling of the bubbles as he broke the surface, and then he could feel the warm breath of air on his flank that brought with it an exciting mixture of comfort and fear. He splashed like a rock back into the water, having caught the briefest glimpse of the world above. "Yeehaaa…!" he shouted as he swam down to prepare for another lunge upwards. "Come on, Una, leap with me!" he shouted. But Una had already performed a perfect 'rainbow leap' and was preparing for her next attempt when a small silvery shape leapt out of the water in front of her and a small "Yippeee!" could be heard before the shape plopped with an awkward splash back into the water.

"Brynjar?" laughed Salto.

The little smolt lunged into the air and wobbled through a demented arc in the air. He landed awkwardly beside Salto. "What do you think? Was I any good?"

"You were fine, but what are you doing up here? You should be out at sea with the other smolts."

Brynjar looked shyly at Salto: "I wasn't sure about leaving the river. I felt safer with you bigger fish." And then, in an attempt to change the subject, he added, "This leaping is such fun. Come on, jump with me... please?"

"I'm not sure that I should, really. I know, we'll do three jumps and then you must be on your way. Is that a deal?"

"Yes, yes... now, you go first and I'll copy you."

Brynjar jumped several times, each as bad as his first attempt, and each time Salto paused to tell the smolt it was time to stop, he pleaded, "Just one more, please?"

Finally, when Brynjar had completed two orderly jumps in succession, Salto turned to the smolt and said,

"Come on, Shrimp, it is time for you to go."

"One more…?"

"No, it's time to go. You mustn't be afraid of the way ahead. Look, there's a group of smolts gathering over there. You can swim with them down to the sea."

Salto took Brynjar to join the others, who greeted the small smolt with happy laughter.

A little while after, the sun sank to just above the horizon and the air above the river cooled. Long patches of shade stretched across the Tern Pool as the splashes of leaping Hofsin became less frequent. Salto was tiring and decided to end his play with one last enormous lunge to see how high he could leap above the surface. He broke through the surface film, elated by the bubbles and air, and tingled with the chill evening air against his scales. At the top of his leap, just as he was about to fall backwards to the water, he saw a shape that turned his tingles to a shiver. There, beside a rock, crouched the unmistakeable and sinister shape of a Shadow.

Salto swam at once to tell Storlax what he had seen. He found his chief resting behind a large rock at the bottom of the pool.

"So, Salto, did you enjoy it?"

"Yes, I did. But, Storlax, in my last leap I saw a Shadow hiding beside a rock."

"They will be everywhere we go, Salto. When we rest during the day, we should always keep to the deeper, darker corners of the river. We should only swim upstream at night, when the Shadows have gone to rest. If we do this, then there is not much they can do to harm us." Rocky drifted down and Storlax made a space for him. "Ah, there you are my friend. Come, rest here with me in this quiet place and meet young Salto. He is one of our finest young Hofsin."

Rocky nodded at Salto and Storlax saw that the young Hofsin was embarrassed to be in the company of his King and to be given such praise.

"Now you mustn't be shy, Salto. You are with friends and family. What you have learnt today will prepare you for the Great Falls that lie ahead of us. Why, Rocky here is a legend. Many Great Journeys ago, when the river was in full flood and no Hofsin, not even I, would dare brave them, it was Rocky who led the way with the mightiest leap ever seen..."

Salto looked over at Rocky in admiration but Rocky seemed uncomfortable with the praise he was receiving. He looked away as Storlax continued.

"… and see that scar on his head. That was the price he paid for his valour. Without that one leap, that year's Great Journey would never have been completed. As I said, he's a legend, Salto, and I know that one day you, too, will have tales told about you!"

The Glimmer

The Hofsin rested in the Tern Pool. Above, the wind blew warm summery rain. Luscious raindrops dimpled the surface of the river. The sun had not shone for several days and the shoal felt newly safe in their selected lies. Una and Salto lay contentedly in a shaded trough to one side of the river, where they listened to the patter of the rain from above and enjoyed the soft buffeting of the current as it slid over their sleek bodies.

Una watched as Salto rested and then noticed a brief glimmer that swept past them in the distance. Salto noticed it as well and roused himself from his torpor.

A short while later, there it was again: a glittering, sparkly, glistening black-and-silver glimmer, which swept a few metres in front of them before disappearing downstream and away.

"I don't like the look of that, Salto. Let's swim away," said Una.

"It's nothing. As long as we stay here we'll be fine," replied Salto, who was still only half awake.

Again the glittering object swept past them; this time it was only a metre away. Una flinched and retreated behind the rock, while Salto looked on in curiosity. This time he could make out different colours of black, silver and a flash of blue. It looked like a small fish.

"Now, why would that tiddler approach me? He should be swimming away," Salto thought to himself. He was about to turn away to swim with Una when again, the glimmer swept close and fast. This time it almost hit him on his nose.

Una looked and saw Salto's eyes flash and his mouth open, his teeth bared. She yelled, "No! Leave it!"

But it was too late, for Salto had snapped at it and caught the glimmer in his mouth. He turned away and downwards, as he always did when he ate a fish, but he was suddenly stopped and hauled sideways. The object concealed a hook that sank into the corner of his mouth, and the line that was attached to it was pulled hard from above. Salto looked in alarm at Una.

Salto was at first puzzled as to what was happening. He tried to cough out the fly but it was lodged in his mouth. At first he leant against the pressure that was pulling him towards the bank, then he decided to swim to the safety of the deeper water. He bored deep, taking with him the line from above. He was nearing a group of boulders when the line was pulled hard from above. He realised that he would have to fight to free himself, to flee away from whatever was at the other end of the line.

He could picture Storlax leaping and twisting, and knew that he must do the same. Summoning all of his strength he bored deeper and then turned to lunge at the surface. He erupted through the water and twisted and flipped for all his worth, sometimes leaping forwards, sometimes plunging sideways down onto the line that had him in its grasp. Never had a Hofsin fought so hard. Through the blur of action he saw two Shadows standing on the bank, one smaller than the other. Salto's panic turned to chill fear. Una looked on in horror as she saw Salto struggle against the line that was now pulling him through the water. She was helpless.

"How did this happen?" Storlax, who had swum to join her, asked gravely.

"It all happened so quickly, he just snapped at it. It seemed so harmless. What can we do, Storlax? What can we do?"

"Nothing…" murmured Storlax. "Nothing. He is lost to us now." Storlax turned and sank back to the safety of his lie. "We have lost our prince… Our prince is gone."

Una was too concerned for Salto to understand the full meaning of what Storlax had said.

Salto composed himself and worked out what he must do. He had heard how Hofsin had escaped from lines and Shadows by using the fast-flowing water to double their strength. He decided to swim downstream and leap over the lip of the Tern Pool. He felt certain that would free him. But first he turned and swam straight towards the Shadows and the line went slack. He had caught them by surprise. Then he splashed and turned in the faster water and then thrashed his tail for all he was worth. He ran headlong downstream, hurtling past other Hofsin and over rocks and boulders. He could sense the pressure build towards the end of the pool, he could almost hear the roar of the falls. He prepared himself for the great leap into the air and freedom.

The line tightened and he was hauled back, just as his nose teetered on the edge of the falls. He had little strength left and he was hauled steadily but surely towards the bank.

Una looked on helplessly as she saw her brave Salto pulled towards the gravelly bank. She swam closer and saw his tired body roll over on to its side as the Shadow reached in to pluck him out of the water.

Salto was gone. The Shadows had taken him.

———

Imagine you are on the bank of the river on that fine sunny day and hear the only human words that are spoken in our story…

"*We'll release this fish,*" says the father to his son.

The father has fished this river for many years and loves the river and the animals that live around it, as he loves his own home. Never before has he seen a salmon fight with such vigour and courage. Never has he seen such jumps, and never before has he felt such a strong urge to see a fish put back in the water – to return it unharmed to continue the Great Journey.

He shows his son how to hold the salmon in the water, to be sure to wet his hands before touching it, so as not to burn the fish's skin. He shows the boy how to remove the hook from the corner of its mouth; the task is made easier because they have already broken the barbs from their hooks. He photographs the fish while the boy holds it in the water. A souvenir for life of a titanic struggle on a special day.

After a short while the salmon's gills open and close more regularly, and the man whispers for his son to release the fish. At first the fish drifts downwards but, when it senses that it is free to swim away, it swipes its tail twice and disappear to the deepest part of the pool. The salmon is free.

The father and son sit on the bank to talk about the great struggle that they have just encountered. Soon they stop talking and listen instead to the song of the whimbrels, the cries of the terns and the drumming of the snipe. The sun now shines in a billowy sky down onto the grassy bank where they sit – it seems as if the whole of nature is celebrating this summer's day.

———

A few metres away, in the Tern Pool, Salto swam free.

"Salto, is that you?" Una swam to greet him. "How did you escape? I saw the Shadows take you. We all thought you were gone forever. Are you all right?"

Salto was still breathing heavily, but was soon his usual, chirpy self again. "I'm fine, just a bit tired. It all happened so quickly. I thought it was all over too. But they put me back. The Shadows put me back!"

"You must go and tell Storlax," Una said.

Salto feared that he would be given a telling off for snapping at the glimmer and was not sure that he wanted to go and see Storlax. "Umhh, I'm not sure, Una. Why don't you and I get out of this pool and swim to somewhere safer?"

"I saw salt in his eyes when he saw you caught by the Shadows. He just turned and slowly sank to the depths of the pool. There was no one who could console him. Not even Rocky. Salto, you must see Storlax, you must tell him what has happened."

"Oh, all right then," Salto said, as he swam to the darkest corner of the pool to find Storlax.

Una was right, Storlax greeted Salto with happiness and relief. It was as if a great weight had been lifted from the chief's back. "My dear boy, I really thought that we had lost you forever. How did you escape?"

Salto was about to tell Storlax that he had bit the Shadow on the hand and fought his way to freedom; it would have been a good story and no one would have known that it didn't happen. Instead, when he saw the look of relief and affection on Storlax's face, he knew he could only tell the truth.

"The strangest thing happened. I was helpless in the Shadow's hands and was waiting for the worst. But instead, they took the glimmer from my mouth and then they held me in the water. Next they captured the sun in their hands and flashed it at me. Then, when I had recovered my breath, they released me to swim away."

Storlax thought for a while. "Well, I have never heard of this before. Are you sure this is what happened to you?"

"Absolutely."

"We'll talk more about this as you and I swim to the Raven's Pool. There is much for us to talk about, young Salto. Much for us to talk about."

"What happens at the Raven's Pool?" Salto asked.

"The Parliament of the Animals. And it falls upon me, as King of the Hofsin, to attend the gathering and tell the salmon's tale." He looked at Salto and said solemnly, "You will be there with me, as I was with the Storlax before me. You, Salto of the Hofsin, will be the next Storlax when I die. You need to know these things. You need to prepare yourself, to rise to the challenge of one day leading the Hofsin. Your life is no longer your own, for you now have responsibilities to the clan."

Salto heard these words but hardly understood what they really meant. "I hope that I will be equal to the challenge," he said.

Storlax's eyes twinkled with love, pride and affection. "You will, my boy. You will."

The Parliament of the Animals

And so, all the animals gathered at the Raven's Pool for the Parliament of the Animals. The Eagle was their president. He perched on Eagle Rock, which had been used by the parliament for over a thousand years. It was the Eagle who had soared the mountains and valleys long before the Shadows had arrived to inhabit this land. It was the Eagle who flew higher than any other bird, it was the Eagle who travelled far and wide across the land, and it was the Eagle who had suffered most at the hands of the Shadows. It was the Eagle who called the first parliament all those years ago, shortly after the Shadows settled the land.

To his left perched his closest advisor, the Raven. It was the Raven who lived amongst the Shadows and who possessed magical powers that were a match for the Shadows and their ways. The Raven could understand the Shadows' language and knew of their inner sadness.

To his right perched the Tern. It was the Tern who each year travelled thousands of miles from the southern tip of the globe, to nest and breed in this country. For years the Tern had observed the Shadows of other countries on his long journey and was their fiercest critic in the parliament; he had seen what they had done elsewhere and would fight with all his might to stop them.

The sun had sunk below the hills, leaving the sky a pale blue, streaked with the softest of clouds. A gentle breeze riffled through the grass and ruffled, from time to time, the feathers on Eagle's body. In front of him, he could see the Mink, the Swan, the Fox, the Whimbrel, the Snipe, the Hawk, the Plover and all the animals and birds that lived in and visited this country. He watched them as they stood beside the river, and listened to their voices carried gaily on the breeze, a happy murmur of talk and chatter. And beyond, in the river itself, swam the Duck and the Goose with the Charr, the Trout, the Eel and the Sea Trout.

The great gathering was complete; the Parliament of the Animals was about to take place.

"Ladies and Gentlemen, order please!" Raven's croaking voice brought silence to the gathering. The only sound to be heard was the whispering of the breeze through the grass and the murmuring of the river. "Are we all here?"

———

Storlax and Salto had been delayed above the rapids by a group of Shadows who had fished late into the evening. The setting sun had made a menacing shade across the river and they were dangling all manner of articles into the river, all with sharp hooks and barbs. Storlax had decided that they could not risk being caught, so he and Salto lay in a dark lie, ignoring the gleaming spinning objects that tried to tempt them.

At length, the Shadows left and Storlax and Salto moved on as fast as they could. They rounded the bend and were greeted by Great Northern Diver, who landed noisily in the water beside them. "Storlax, how good to see you, my old friend!"

"Good to see you too, Loon. I was just thinking that it wouldn't be too long before Tern sent someone to find us, and here you are! Well met, well met."

"Is all well?" Loon saw how much Storlax had aged.

"None of us are getting any younger, old friend. You haven't met Salto here. He is here as my aide. Now, what news?"

"Eagle apologises for starting without you, but there is much to discuss. The Shadows are up to no good. There are Shadows and their machines everywhere. It is very bad, the Shadows are moving the very mountains themselves and even redirecting the rivers. Tern tells us that he has seen this all before in other countries and that the Shadows will soon flood whole areas. Homes will be lost, nesting sites destroyed. Even Mink is upset about it. We have to make plans to evacuate. Raven is plotting dark revenge. I'll swim along beside you and tell you more as we travel. It is very bad news, Storlax. Very bad indeed."

Salto did not say a word as he swam along behind Storlax but he listened to every word that was spoken and became sadder by the mile as he heard the stories of the Shadows' greed and stupidity.

There was a heated debate at the Raven's Pool when Storlax, Salto and Loon arrived. Virtually every animal had sad tales to tell of their encounters with Shadows and Tern, along with the other migratory birds, added fuel to the fire by describing what they had witnessed in other countries.

Falcon, who was rather envious of Eagle's authority and had no time for his ponderous wisdom, demanded action.

"Now is the time to act. We cannot wait any longer and sit and watch our country and our fellow animals destroyed in this way. We must unleash the full power of the ravens against the Shadows and we must do it swiftly! What say you, Raven?"

Raven paused and looked at Eagle before he spoke. Eagle nodded in encouragement. "It is true. The Shadows become worse each year, but it is not as easy as Falcon suggests. The Shadows are fast becoming a sad breed. We ravens live amongst them and we have seen them change over the years. In winters past, they would gather to work, sing and play together. Now we see them sitting looking at their boxes of light in their homes. They throw away food and have become idle. It is sad to see those who have been given so much by nature, squander and fritter it away."

Storlax and Salto listened with all the animals to Raven's words.

"But surely you can act against them, Raven?" asked Tern.

"Raven's powers are dark, mysterious and above all – secret, Tern. They are not for us to order or command," said Eagle.

A small clear voice spoke from the back of the gathering. "It is not all bad news…"

It was Ptarmigan who spoke, but her words were soon lost in the noise made by Mink and Tern, who shouted, "The Shadows nowadays do only bad. We cannot trust them!" Eagle flashed a look at Mink and Tern that brought them both to order and they muttered apologies. "Continue please, Ptarmigan. What have you seen?"

"This year, for the first time in many a while, the Shadows have not hunted us down with their thundersticks. They left us to winter in safety, and this spring we have hatched more chicks than in a long while."

Eagle nodded his head and asked the gathering, "Are there any other stories like this?"

Storlax moved closer to the bank to rest on the gravel bank where Storlaxes for many generations had addressed the parliament. His dorsal fin stood erect into the air.

"We have seen much over the years to give us grave concern from the Shadows. They have poisoned our rivers. Their Nets of the Dead pollute the seabed and send millions of sea lice to damage our young fish. They have taken us from the rivers when we swim on our Great Journey to breed and increase our stock. But just yesterday something happened that I have never seen before. Young Salto here was taken by the Shadows. We thought he was gone, but then he was put back into the river unharmed. It was a remarkable moment and it made me think that perhaps some of the Shadows know that they cannot keep taking us from the river."

Storlax's story caused much muttering and talk, which was again silenced by a glance of Eagle's eye.

Eagle turned to Snowy Owl, who was sitting in the shadows behind him. Owl was the most mystical of all the creatures and had the powers of divination and prophecy. He combined these powers to use as wisdom for the parliament. Eagle did not need to ask him a question, for Owl knew already what Eagle was thinking. In a spectral, haunting voice, Owl addressed the parliament; he did not raise his voice, for all could hear his ghostly words.

"We, wild Feather, Fin and Fur, we know that we eat only what we need, we kill only that which we have to. We can live side by side. We always have, we always will. The Shadows used to be like us but now they take away and do not put back. It is not the time for Raven to use his powers against them, for nature will take its own revenge and the Shadows will pay in their own way when the time comes. The news from the country is most distressing but we have always seen change. Ptarmigan's and Storlax's stories are some of many where we see the Shadows doing good things. Eagle and Falcon, you have seen them defend your nests and you have no problems with thundersticks any more."

Snowy Owl looked and blinked, for his thoughts made him weary. The breeze had gone and only the river could be heard.

"We Feathers, we have our wings and we can fly away to another land. It has always been thus. But this is a good land and we must stay. I see a time in the future, a time when the Shadows can learn of their folly and we can live easily with them once again…"

And with those last words, Snowy Owl beat his wings and vanished into the sky.

"Owl has spoken and I agree with him," said Eagle. "My decision is that there will be no action this year against the Shadows, but we will keep a watchful eye upon them and when we meet next year, we will see how they have progressed."

Eagle looked around him and laughed a throaty laugh. "Now come on, this has been enough talk! Let us mingle and enjoy this day when we can all speak at peace with one another. We have journeyed far and have much to say. We must also say our farewells to those who will not be with us again. It is time to enjoy our fellowship."

Storlax and Salto were some of the last to leave the Great Gathering, for many wished to say their farewells to Storlax. These were not sad farewells, they were happy and cheerful, for all animals know that each parting may be the last.

Storlax was pleased that Salto had seen the parliament and knew in his heart that the young Hofsin would make a fine king when his time came.

"Never fear, Storlax, we will keep a kind and watchful eye on young Salto for you. Go gently now, go gently," said Eagle, as Storlax and Salto swam on to join the Hofsin to tell them the news of the Parliament of the Animals.

To the Foss Pool

And the sun shone over the land.

Each day it shone, from early morn to late evening; bright, unrelenting, burning sun whose rays brightened the darkest corners of the river bed. It had not rained for many a day, causing the water in the river to lower dramatically, exposing rocks and features that were normally hidden under water. As the river level sank, the water temperature rose. The Shadows arrived with the dawn and only left the river after the sun had sunk beyond the hills, sometimes staying until darkness.

The Hofsin had become edgy and nervous; some had fallen back downstream to seek more sheltered pools but the bulk lay restless in the bright stewy water, wanting to go neither forward nor backward. They found what cover they could, but the sun and the low, hot water combined to make them feel exposed and vulnerable. In these conditions, the Hofsin became easy prey for the Shadows.

"This will never do," Storlax confided to Rocky. They lay shaded by the trickling remnants of a side-stream's waterfall, which provided them shelter and some much-needed oxygen. "Each day it gets worse, Rocky. We are losing too many Hofsin to the Shadows. I've never seen the river like this before, and I've never seen such a dispirited clan – some are even talking about abandoning the Great Journey itself. I can't let that happen, I just can't let that happen, I have to get them onwards and over the Great Falls to the Home Pool. It is my duty."

Storlax waited for a reply, but none came.

"I said, 'it is my duty to do so!'" Storlax repeated.

"I heard you, Storlax. I heard you. I'm thinking. I find it hard to think and talk at the same time," Rocky replied and then added brightly, "I'm going for a swim. I'm fed up with hiding under here, cowering like an eel. Time for Rocky to take a swim."

And with these words, Rocky propelled his enormous body to the middle and most exposed part of the pool.

There, he sashayed in the shallow water, his silvery flanks in full view to Shadows and every passing bird and animal. He lay there humming and muttering to himself with not a care in the world.

Salto and Una swam forwards to join Storlax. "What's he doing? The Shadows are bound to see him. He'll get caught out there. Is he mad?" said Una.

"I've long ago stopped trying to understand our friend Rocky. He is a law unto himself. What's he doing? I cannot say, but whatever it is, don't any of you dare think of joining him!"

A bright red-and-golden glimmer, thrown by a Shadow, was soon swirling its way towards where Rocky lay. Rocky seemed unaware of it as it swung a few feet in front of him. Again it came, this time brushing the tip of his nose. Una and Salto both gasped while Storlax looked on in bewilderment. "What is he up to?" he whispered loudly.

"Be careful Rocky, please," urged Una.

But Rocky was heedless. He hummed and murmured a tuneless ditty as, time and time again, the glimmer passed tantalisingly close.

Word spread like a torrent throughout the Hofsin, many of whom overcame their fear to see what was going on.

"Please be careful," willed Salto as the glimmer started yet another pass in front of Rocky's impassive face. When it had passed, Rocky slipped backwards to a swirling eddy beside a rock. A sigh of relief could be heard from all the Hofsin who had gathered to witness the event.

"Well, thank goodness, he's come to his senses," said Una.

"I'd not be so sure…" replied Salto, as the glimmer plopped into the water just in front of Rocky's new lie, where it wallowed and wafted in the eddy until it was dangling tantalisingly in front of the seemingly oblivious Rocky. For what seemed like minutes, it hovered in front of him. And then, to everyone's complete astonishment, Rocky swam forward and let it brush over the scar on his head. He then edged further forwards and nudged the glimmer from side to side with his brow.

"Storlax, stop him. They'll take him. I know they will," said Salto, whose memory of the Shadows was only too fresh in his mind.

"Rocky knows what he is doing. We should all take comfort from the contempt he is showing the Shadows," replied Storlax, but his words hid the true fear he was feeling.

The Hofsin let out another communal gasp as Rocky idly opened his mouth and, in one mighty gulp, swallowed the glimmer whole. Just as all the Hofsin were about to shout "No Rocky!" and before the Shadow on the bank could react, Rocky blew it out again, as if it were a feather in the breeze.

There was stunned silence from all the Hofsin.

Rocky turned to face them and, with the laziest of smiles, said "The Shadows hate it when I do that!" He laughed as the glimmer was dragged away and out of the water by the Shadow.

Storlax looked at his Hofsin. He could see a gleam once again return to their noble eyes. He seized his opportunity.

"Follow me, my Hofsin! We must ignore the sun's rays. We must ignore glimmers that the Shadows cast in our path. On this day we are impervious to them. Let's make haste to the Foss Pool, where we can shelter and make ready for the Great Falls. Swim fast, swim fast and follow me. Swim as only Hofsin know how!"

Soon, all the Hofsin in the river had heard the call and prepared to set off upstream to the gorge where the Foss Pool awaited them.

Salto was about to paddle forward with the rest of the shoal, when he heard a young voice. "Wow! Did you see that? That was incredible. But we must never do it ourselves, must we?" It was Brynjar, who had a little cluster of small fry around him.

"What are you doing here? You should have gone to sea long ago." Salto was astonished. "And who are all these little folk with you?"

"Ah, I'm glad you asked me that," replied Brynjar, trying to keep the embarrassment out of his voice. "I did try to go, honestly, but I just didn't feel ready to leave the river. None of the adult fish wanted to talk to me so, when I found this shoal of small fry, I thought I'd take them under my fin."

"But what are you going to do up here? The summer will end soon and winter will be upon us. You'll never be able to leap the Great Falls. Brynjar can't stay here, can he, Rocky?" Salto asked of the giant fish, who had drifted over to join them.

"Well, if he tucks himself away in a sheltered eddy, he should come to no harm," replied Rocky and then in a kindly voice added, "Young Brynjar, you make sure you take care of these little folk. They shouldn't be out here in the river. Follow me, let's find a sheltered spot where you can keep them out of trouble until we return."

The smolt swam backwards and forwards like a crab guarding his hole. "Brynjar, reporting for duty! I'll keep them out of harm's way, don't you worry."

Salto smiled as he said goodbye and paddled hard so that he could catch up with Una. Together they swam to the Foss Pool that lay at the foot of the Great Falls.

The Great Falls

The Great Falls were created thousands of years ago, when the land cooled and the very rocks themselves moved and cracked, leaving a steep rocky precipice over which the river tumbled and boiled as it made its way to the sea. The water had gouged a deep hole at the bottom of the drop and it was here, at the Foss Pool, where the Hofsin gathered before leaping up through the cascading water to a smooth and slippery treacherous slab of rock. The Hofsin called this rock the 'Block of Destiny', from where they could slither their way upwards to the Home Pool. Most salmon could leap onto the Block of Destiny, but only a very few fish were able to leap onto the block and swim their way into the Home Pool on their first attempt. The majority fell back into the pool to try again.

Una and Salto swam into the fast-flowing water that led to the Foss Pool. The water's surface boiled and spumed overhead and the young fish swam swiftly and in safety to the foot of the Falls. What greeted them was a sight of pure chaos.

The river thundered down into the pool from the Falls above, driving water out from the pool in all directions. The deep part of the pool was surrounded by ledges of rock and boulders, some sharp and threatening. Several fish had been blasted to one side by the force of the current. They had been dashed and broken by these rocks and ledges; their corpses were set upon greedily by a family of foxes. The day's truce brought about by the Parliament of the Animals was long over.

The water itself was a vortex of currents, foam and bubbles, in which Hofsin swam and lay in all directions. No sooner had one fish leapt out of the water than he fell back again, with another fish crashing down on his head.

"We'll never get up there, Salto. We'll get crushed and broken against those rocks," Una said.

"Let's just wait a while and watch, Una. The pool is emptying. Some Hofsin must be making it up to the top. Look, here's Storlax."

Storlax looked at his Hofsin as he had the night they set forth on the Great Journey.

"This night your skills will be put to the ultimate test. For you will leap the Great Falls and then you will find the Block of Destiny. It is here that you must fight your hardest. Only when you have cleared this treacherous obstacle can you reach the Home Pool. There, safe from the Shadows, we will be able to rest and mend."

He used the Great Journey's summoning call.

"It is time! It... is... time!" Storlax boomed.

Salto and Una watched as their chief swam to the depths of the pool and then hurled himself upwards. They could hear his mighty roar above the commotion in the pool: "Follow me...!" And with those words Storlax's huge tail slapped into the surface water and was gone. Other fish followed his lead, and even those who had failed several attempts now had the spirit to succeed.

"Salto, let's go now. I feel I can do it," Una said bravely, although she was still not sure.

"Good for you. We can do this. I know we can. You leap first and I'll follow up behind you," urged Salto.

Una started her lunge to the surface but was stopped when Rocky's giant bulk came tumbling down onto her. They both groaned loudly.

"I wasn't cut out for this for this sort of jump. I'm better on the journey downstream, if you know what I mean," Rocky said as they regrouped in the foaming turmoil at the base of the Falls. "I'm not sure that I can make it in this low water."

Una looked back at him with a 'you can do it' expression on her face. Newly encouraged, he paused, turned, swam to the bottom and then shot his quivering body through the water and out of the pool.

"Come on Salto, Rocky may need our help to get over the Block of Destiny." And with these words she set off to make her lunge.

Salto followed close behind her. He could feel the rush of air and water against his flanks, hear the thunder in the water. It felt as if the weight of the whole river was pressing down upon him. And, just as he felt that he was about to fall back into the pool, he landed on the Block of Destiny. He could see Una, wriggling as hard as she could across the water that skimmed and swirled over the slab towards them. Ahead of her, he could just make out Rocky's silhouette slithering back towards them across the treacherous slab. Una swam forwards to block his path and not longer after Salto swam to Rocky's other side. They wriggled and struggled to keep his bulk from falling backwards.

"Come on, Rocky, you can do it," urged Una. They were all beginning to weaken; it seemed that the force of the water and the tilt of the rock were going to defeat them. There they remained, battling against the force of gravity and the tumble of the current.

In the midst of all this turmoil, Salto became aware of two tiny black eyes staring at him from the rocks beside the falls. In the most cold and threatening way, they seemed to be saying, "We'll meet again". The eyes caused a shiver to run through his entire body. He strained to see more clearly through the spray and find out to whom the eyes belonged, but they had become shrouded in the splashy shower. A shout from Una brought his attention back to the weighty matter of Rocky.

"One last effort everybody!"

And with these final words of encouragement, they pushed and paddled for all they were worth, until they edged over the top of the slab and slipped into the calmer water on the top of the Block of Destiny. They had reached the top.

Una, Salto and Rocky felt the chill wind of morning on their backs as they dropped, exhausted, over the lip and into the safety of the Home Pool.

The Home Pool

The sun rose behind the mountains, casting a light that glimmered on the water, sending soft beams to where Storlax lay at the bottom of the Home Pool, his head resting against a patch of weed. This was the fourth time that he had leapt the Great Falls, no other salmon in the Hofsin's history had ever achieved as many. He was the biggest and oldest of the Hofsin and yet he had managed to drive his body up and over the Great Falls. The King was weary to his bones. He let the weed wash to and fro in the current across his scales. The fronds soothed the old wounds that had been opened by the battering his body had received from the Great Falls. One of his fins had been torn away in the ascent. He ignored the pain, realising with darker sadness that this would be the last time he would be capable of leading his Hofsin over the Great Falls.

As he regained some of his strength, he willed himself to swim to visit the Hofsin, who had gathered during the night in the Home Pool. He tilted his body to one side to compensate for his absent fin and, in this manner, he limped the length and depth of the pool, stopping to speak and give words of encouragement and comfort to his kinsmen. The Great Falls had taken a heavy toll on the Hofsin. They lay in scattered groups, many still out of breath from the leap. Storlax noticed that there were some familiar faces that were missing and knew that he would not see many fellow travellers of earlier journeys again. He sighed as only a king can sigh.

But in his sadness he knew that there were heroic deeds to recognise and congratulations to be given to those who had overcome this, the most difficult of all challenges. He swam to find Salto and Una, for word had reached him that these two young Hofsin alone had leapt the Great Falls on their first attempt, and while helping Rocky.

"Well done, you two," Storlax said as he approached Una and Salto. "Well done!" The two young Hofsin turned to look at their King. They both smiled modestly. They noticed the wound on Storlax's flank and saw the sorry state of the fish around them. They too had hardly any energy left. "Now you must rest and heal. You have overcome the most daunting challenge in the Great Journey and you have helped our dear friend, Rocky. Rest safely in the knowledge that we need go no further upstream. The rock walls that surround our Home Pool will keep us safe from the Shadows now."

Storlax was about to swim away when he noticed Rocky, resting with his head buried in a mound of the softest weed, his huge tail in outline against the pale-green strands.

"Rocky, are you all right?' Storlax asked. There was no reply. Rocky lay motionless.

"He's just tired, like all of us," said Una. "He seemed sad though, when he tucked himself away there. He hasn't spoken for a while."

"I won't disturb him now, but please ask him to come to me when he has rested." He thought for a while and then added, "This is a difficult time for him. Ah well. We mustn't dwell…"

Storlax winced as he turned to swim on to talk to another pod of Hofsin. His whole spine ached from the exertion of the leap. "I'm getting old," he said and he finned away to give comfort and congratulations to others.

It was some time before Rocky stirred. He floated upwards away from the weed and turned to face Una. "Thank you for what you did. I'd still be down there at the bottom of the Falls with Brynjar." He sighed a slow deep sigh and then added, "Perhaps it would be better if I were…"

"Now you mustn't say that. We're all tired, but we're safe here and we will soon mend," soothed Una.

"And it's about time we found you a young Hofsin to nest with," jested Salto.

Rocky slowly nodded his head, his eyes made awkward focus on the pebbly bottom. "No, no nests for Rocky…"

Salto asked, "Why not? You're a fine figure of a salmon, make no mistake. It's why we're here; it's why we've travelled the Great Journey."

Rocky paused for a moment. He had become so used to the story about his heroism on the Great Falls that he had almost come to believe it himself. And realising this again made him even more sad. "You need to know the truth. The story about me shooting the Great Falls and banging my head isn't true. It's a story that Storlax has made up to protect me. I'd like to tell you the truth, so that you know who Rocky really is."

Salto and Una floated silently in front of him as he recounted his tale.

He told them how he was raised not in a river, like other wild salmon, but in one of the Nets of the Dead. He had been raised by the Shadows in a place of horror and sorrow.

"You mean you're a Nameless?" asked Salto. Rocky managed a smile and told him that yes, he was a Nameless. He, like all the other Nameless, was fed food that made him grow bigger and more quickly than normal salmon.

Rocky continued to explain that on a certain day the nets were emptied and the Shadows took the Nameless, one by one, to slaughter them. They used a machine that sparked like summer lightning, which they placed against each Nameless head and that was it. A life over.

Rocky's voice was almost a whisper as it wavered, close to tears.

Una was too shocked to speak. She sidled over to Rocky and blew soft bubbles across his brow to comfort him.

"How did you get out? Did you lead an escape?" Salto asked.

Rocky told of how when it was his turn, just as the spark flashed against his head, the Shadow lost his grip and Rocky slithered back into the sea. He was a free salmon. But the spark had damaged his head and hurt his eye. He rolled it expressionlessly to make the point. At first he was thrilled to be free, to swim unpolluted seawater, but he was an outcast and he soon became lonely. He was shunned and despised by all the wild salmon that he met in the estuary. The young ones teased him for his slow reactions and unusual shape. He tried to chase smaller fish to eat, but he wasn't used to fishing and he soon became hungry. Although he had gained his freedom, he was a prisoner of his loneliness.

"But how did you meet Storlax? How come you know the Hofsin so well?" asked Una.

Rocky told them how when he was at his most lonely, when he was close to starvation and was so desperate that he wished the Shadow's lightning spark had been true: at that darkest of all moments, a shoal of Hofsin came through on their Great Journey. They were led by a different Storlax who ordered his Hofsin to ignore

Rocky. But one young salmon, a Hofsin called Solo who was on his second Great Journey, took pity on him and spent some hours helping him to feed. It was the first act of kindness that Rocky had ever experienced. A tear formed in his eye as he told the tale.

Eventually Solo had to leave with his clan, but he promised that he would find Rocky when he returned to the sea. He took him to a place where a fish called Red Belly lived, a place where he would have a friend.

"I know him," Salto laughed. "He helped me too. He taught me his trick!" This brought a smile to Rocky's face and an end to his tears. He continued in a brighter mood.

During the long winter Rocky stayed with Red Belly, two outcasts who took strength from each other. Rocky learnt to fend for himself. He fed himself as much as he could and he grew and grew. His tattered fins, a legacy from the Nets, slowly mended and after several moons he was a gigantic salmon, not the most attractive but certainly the strongest in the sea who, if he chose, could be the match of any. But Rocky held no such thoughts. The Shadow's lightning spark had erased all aggression and anger from his mind. He was as harmless as he was huge.

Solo was as good as his word. When winter came to an end, and the Hofsin returned to the estuary, he came to Red Belly's lie to find Rocky. Solo, too, had transformed for, on the Hofsin's Great Journey, the Storlax had been caught and taken from the river by the Shadows. Solo had been made the new Storlax in his place. Solo was now King of the Hofsin. He told Rocky that he should join the Hofsin on their way to the feeding grounds, that Rocky was welcome to swim the seas with them. Not all the Hofsin agreed with this, as they despised the Nameless, but Storlax insisted and commanded that, in future, Rocky was to be treated as a wild salmon. He even concocted the story about Rocky bashing his head on the Great Falls to protect him from the abuse and prejudice of the other clans. It was Storlax who gave him the name Rocky.

And so Rocky swam with the Hofsin but, however kind and welcoming they were under the new Storlax's leadership, Rocky knew in his heart that he could never be one of them. Armed with his new identity and his formidable strength, he swam the seas of the Northern Atlantic; he became a nomad of the oceans, experiencing adventures and witnessing sights that no salmon had ever experienced before.

He swam with the killer whales off Greenland, he journeyed to the Sargasso Sea with the eels on their migration and frolicked with shoals of tuna in the warm waters off Africa. He left behind all memories of the Nets of the Dead and the Shadows. He was Rocky, a free citizen of the seas, a cousin of all the Fins that swim the oceans. From humble beginnings he had become a favoured child of the Deep.

But, when spring came each year, the call to make the Great Journey would come. He had no desire to nest but, although he tried to fight it, the call to run rivers and leap Great Falls was one that he couldn't resist.

And so each year he returned to the feeding grounds to join a clan. He was still a Nameless and therefore he had no Home Scent and no home river to return to. He relied instead on the leadership of others. His favourite clan was the Hofsin.

"I was looking for Storlax when I found you in the Straxin river, Una. I had gone the wrong way," said Rocky as he finished his tale. "And very pleased I am that I did find you."

"But why are you sad?" asked Salto.

"Well, for all my adventures and travels, for all the kindness and friendship shown to me by the clans, at this time of year when everyone is nesting I remember who I really am – a Nameless. I realise that I have no family, no clan." His head nodded slowly and his damaged eye teared with sadness.

"Well you've got us, Rocky, and we won't leave you, will we Salto?" said Una as she blew more bubbles of comfort across his brow.

"No, we most certainly won't. You're stuck with us, Rocky, whether you like it or not!"

Rocky smiled his slow Rocky smile. His lazy eye twitched with new happiness.

He had found a home.

Ferox

The gorge was silent except for the 'craak-craak' of Raven, carried by the wind that blew down from the North. His call swirled and echoed mournfully through the rocky outcrops. The long days of summer were far behind – winter was on its way. Each day became shorter than the last, and the sun clung ever more closely to the horizon as the Fur that lived above prepared for the harsher weather. Ice began to form at the edges of the river. With each day that passed the days grew colder and the ice spread until it covered the entire surface. The thickening cover muted the light in the river below and, with it, disappeared the threats from the Shadows; the Hofsin were sealed safely below the surface. They had not eaten for many moons and their once muscular bodies were now gaunt and spare. But they ignored their hunger and the urge to swim back to the sea; instead they remained in the Home Pool to guard their nests, where time lost all meaning for them as they lay under the winter's ice. They rested in the twilight world of winter's trance, their hearts' slow beats measuring the time until the thaw would come and they would head for the sea once again.

Una and Salto lay together beside their nest, happy in the knowledge that in front of them lay thousands of tiny Hofsin who would, in years to come, grow to be fine salmon. And there, in the Home Pool, they enjoyed the deepest contentment a Hofsin can know, for they were now resting beside a nest full of eggs which were the future of the clan. Rocky lay with them. He had not left their side once. For the first time in his life he felt part of a family. They pictured a time, soon to come, when they would leave the river for the sea – a time when they would swim the warm currents and feed their fill once more.

Salto heard Storlax's familiar rumble of a voice, which woke him from his trance. Salto had not seen his King for a while, and he was surprised to see how much he had aged. His face looked fierce but his body was haggard and wasted.

"It seems that Una has chosen a good place for her eggs. Away from the ice, in good deep gravel. They should come to no harm there," he said, nodding at Una who was resting. Then, in a low voice so as not to disturb her, he said to Salto, "I have heard word that the old marauder, Ferox, is leading a group of trout from higher upstream and they're on their way down to us. They will be after our nests. We need to send them packing. I can't allow those scoundrels to undo all the great work we have done these last moons."

"But I thought trout were harmless to us?" said Salto.

"Normally they are not a problem. They live and feed in the river and, unlike us, they have food in their bellies. Ferox is their leader. He was once a fine specimen and a friend but now he has grown old and evil." He paused. "Ferox eats his own young and he'll eat ours, too," he whispered bitterly.

"I'll come with you, Storlax. Will we need others to help us?" Salto said.

"Yes, as many as you can find. But we must leave some to guard the nests. If we fail they will be our last defence. And see if you can stir Rocky. Try to get him to come too."

Salto swam over to where Rocky lay in his contented lethargy. He twitched and murmured as if enjoying the happiest dream. "Mmh? What... who is it?" he said, as Salto nudged him back to life. His lazy eye took some while to focus and his whole body shook as he became more aware. "Has the thaw come?" he asked.

"No, not yet. We need your help. Storlax says that Ferox and his tribe are not far away. We have to send them packing. We need you to come with us," urged Salto.

Rocky did not respond for a while and when he did, his words were to disappoint the young Hofsin. "No..." Rocky hesitated. " No... I won't come with you."

"Why not?" Salto was surprised by the giant's reaction.

"I can't..."

"But you must, Rocky. Storlax has asked you."

"Salto, I can't, that's all." Rocky did not want to speak any more about it and looked away sadly.

"We need you, Rocky. We will have to fight Ferox. We're all weak. We haven't fed since the ocean. Look at Storlax over there, he can barely swim in a straight line, and I've never done anything like this before. We need you, Rocky, you're the biggest and strongest by far. You can't let us down. Please come with us. We must fight Ferox's evil away or he'll take our nests."

"Salto, all this I know, but I just can't. I don't have it in me. I don't fight, I can't." Rocky looked at Salto and shook his head sorrowfully. He would not change his mind.

Salto was crestfallen. He tried to hide his disappointment as he turned to swim away to join the others, but he couldn't. He became angry and swirled gravel in Rocky's face as he swam on to join Storlax.

"If we show any weakness they will overrun us. We must appear to be strong even if we don't feel it," Storlax said as, together, the weary band swam upstream.

"No Rocky, I see," he added to Salto, who swam beside him. He could see that Salto was too disappointed to answer. "Well, don't be too hard on him. Since the blow to his head…"

"I know the truth Storlax, Rocky told us about him being a Nameless. He's told us the whole story," Salto said flatly.

"Ah, well. Then you'll understand even more why he doesn't come with us now. It's just not his way."

"But we need him. Doesn't he realise the danger we're all in?"

"Only too well, only too well, Salto. Now forget about Rocky, we have to focus on the task in hand." Storlax pushed forward to lead the cocks onwards. The ice had made the water shallow and the Hofsin became more and more nervous, and it was in growing fear that the band of Hofsin entered the murky twilight of the Rock Pool.

The Hofsin came to rest in the middle of the pool. They looked around anxiously, as Ferox and his crew could be hiding behind the boulders that littered the river bed. Each rock spelt danger. They edged forward in wary silence, a silence that was broken by a sinister, treacly voice.

"Good Evening, Storlax." It was a voice of pure evil. "Now, why don't you all just turn around and go back to the sea and leave us in peace?"

"Where are you, Ferox? Show yourself, you wretched fish!" Storlax boomed. "Come on, show yourself!"

"Don't be so anxious, Storlax. We mean no harm," the voice continued from behind a boulder. "There's no need for any unpleasantness. Why don't you take your Hofsin back to where you belong and leave the river to us?"

"I won't because I can't trust you, Ferox. There was a time when you fed on the flies and the minnows that lived in the river. We were friends then, but you have become black-hearted. You eat your own children and you will do the same to ours if we let you. I have to stop you. I WILL stop you!"

Salto moved to swim fin to fin with Storlax: "Let me go and get him, I'll flush him out."

"No, you wait here," Storlax whispered. "This is something I have to do alone."

Slowly the grotesque form of Ferox emerged from behind the boulder. His body was vastly distended, his head bloated and sinister. His eyes, cold and wicked, were set in deep sockets and his teeth, sharp as needles, protruded menacingly from his ragged mouth. Behind him his band of trout lurked in the gloom.

"You've aged, Storlax. Look at you. You can hardly swim. Are you sure you want to fight here under the ice? Wouldn't you rather go back to your Home Pool?" Ferox goaded.

"Not while you're in my river, Ferox," vowed Storlax. "Not while you remain here. It's time to finish this, once and for all." Summoning all the strength that remained in his battered body, he commanded, "I AM STORLAX, KING OF THE HOFSIN. I CHALLENGE YOU TO THE DEATH, FEROX. TO THE DEATH!"

"Well, that is very sad to hear. And what, pray, are you going to fight me with? You have no teeth, Storlax. You salmon lose them all in the river, don't you? Are you going to 'gum' me to death?" taunted Ferox. Opening his mouth he bared hideous rows of pointed teeth. "This won't take long…" as he spoke he hurled himself at Storlax, snapping, snarling and gnashing his needle teeth. Ferox moved swiftly for one so big, his first attack caught Storlax by surprise and drew blood immediately.

The battle had begun. Two mighty fish had entered combat, but only one would survive.

———

Una became aware that Salto was no longer with her and looked over to where Rocky had sunk his head abjectly into the weed.

"Rocky, where's Salto?" she asked.

"He's gone with Storlax," came the simple reply.

"Why? Is there something wrong?"

Rocky emerged from the weed and turned to face her. "Ferox the cannibal trout is on the move towards us. He is after the Hofsin nests. Storlax took a group to fight them away." Rocky knew what Una's next question would be.

"Well, why didn't they ask you to go with them, Rocky? Surely they'll need your strength?"

"I can't do it, Una."

Una thought for a while, as anger and resentment welled up inside her. "How could you not go, Rocky? Storlax is weak and old. They'll be swimming to their deaths. How could you let them go without you? How could you do that?"

"Because I'm scared, Una. I'm scared to my bones. I can't fight," Rocky moaned. "I'm so scared, Una."

'Well that's not good enough, Rocky! Look in front of us – our nest, the nest that you've watched over. And look around you – hundreds of other nests all the same. The whole future of the Hofsin clan lies in this gravel, Rocky. If Ferox comes here all this will be gone. He and his trout will eat every last egg!"

"I know, I know…" Rocky sighed heavily. "But there's nothing I can do."

Una saw that there was no point in getting more angry with Rocky. He was distressed enough as it was. Instead she talked as calmly to him as she could.

"Look, I know that you are a Nameless and that the Shadow's lightning spark has made you different but, deep down inside your soul, I know that you are salmon. Rocky, do you remember when you came to my rescue, when I was trapped in the Straxin river?"

"Of course I remember," mumbled Rocky.

'Well, it was you who made me think of the Home Scent."

"I know what you are going to say, Una, but I don't have a Home Scent... I don't know the Deep – I'm a broken Nameless."

"Have you tried?"

"Yes."

"I mean have you *really* tried? Please try now, Rocky. We need you to help. Please let you mind go dark and search for the Deep in your soul. Search like you've never tried anything else before. Our Hofsin future relies on you and the Deep!"

"Una, believe me, it won't work. There's nothing to be done." Rocky's huge frame shuddered as he cried with sadness and shame.

"Well, at least swim with me to find them. Will you do that?" snapped Una.

Rocky gave a silent shrug in reply and they both set off upstream.

Nanny Charr

Fish scales and blood swirled in the water as Rocky and Una entered the Rock Pool. Storlax and Ferox were engaged in mortal combat and it was impossible to tell who was winning. One moment, Storlax rammed Ferox brutally against a boulder; so hard was the impact that Ferox screamed out loud. The next, Ferox bit hard and long into Storlax's flank. The King winced visibly but would not cry out as he dived to free himself.

Salto and the other young Hofsin moved to step in but were shouted away by Storlax. "Don't you dare!" As he said this he took another thunderous blow from Ferox that sent him tumbling to the bottom of the pool.

"You must do something, Rocky. You can't let this happen," pleaded Una. But Rocky remained silent.

Below him, Storlax tumbled to the rock-strewn river bed where Ferox struck again with his teeth. They ripped across the flank where Storlax had lost his fin. The King cried out this time, for the pain was so great. His strength was ebbing away from him. He struggled to raise himself. He willed himself to find the strength for one final charge; if it failed he knew it would be his last.

Ferox circled around him, waiting for the opportunity to strike again when, with a mighty roar, Storlax slapped his tail hard against the riverbed and propelled himself upwards and into Ferox's soft belly.

Ferox cried out in fear as he was hurled upwards. He wailed again as his head crashed into the jagged ice ceiling. He screamed aloud as the ice crystals ground into his scales, the brittle hardness burning the very flesh off his back.

Storlax drove the thrashing Ferox as hard as he could, ignoring the screams and shouts from his foe. He knew it was nearly over.

"I surrender! I surrender!" squealed Ferox.

Storlax tried to block Ferox's cries out of his mind. The King was weakening and he knew that this would be his last chance to kill the monster.

"Please let me go, Storlax, I've learnt my lesson. We'll trouble you no more, I swear it," Ferox pleaded with a voice that had found humility. "I swear it. I swear it on the Deep!"

He cried out again as the searing of the ice convulsed through his body once more.

"Don't... trust... him... Storlax" Rocky said as he swam forward, closer to the fray. His heavy voice could be heard through Ferox's cries. "You cannot trust him!"

"You can, you can!" pleaded Ferox. "I'll go upstream to beyond the lake. We'll never return!" Again his body convulsed in agony.

Storlax was tiring, and he knew in his heart that he should let Ferox escape, for he had given his word. He slowly eased the pressure on the rubbery belly of the cannibal trout and soon the two mighty forms drifted downwards to deeper water. Panting heavily they eyed each other.

"Be gone, Ferox. Take your tribe with you. We'll not meet in this life again. Be gone!"

Ferox turned to swim away and, as he did so, Rocky saw an evil glint in his eye. "Watch out!" said Rocky, but it was too late; Ferox struck again. This time his teeth scratched and dug the length of Storlax's face. His one good eye became covered in blood. The King groaned and slumped against the rocks.

Ferox circled slowly, panting and gasping. He eyed Storlax. "You fool, you old fool. You are right, we will not meet again in this life." Ferox opened his mouth and snarled but, as he prepared to deliver the lethal blow, the bulky form of Rocky drifted between the two adversaries. His huge body floated in front of Ferox and, when they were level, Rocky stared coolly into his eyes.

"Go away," Rocky's voice was void of emotion.

"You! The one they call Rocky. What name is that for a salmon? The mongrel Rocky. The half-wit, the fool! Shoo," Ferox goaded.

"Go away," Rocky repeated in the same calm voice. Beneath him, he could see Storlax tumble to the river bed, blood seeping from his wounds. "Go away…"

"Get out of my way, you idiot, or I'll tear you to pieces, too!" Ferox hissed. Rocky edged away slowly, his head pointed downwards.

"That's it, you oaf. Go back to your Nameless friends in the Nets. You have no reason to be here with real fish. Paddle away, you freak of nature." Ferox provoked as he prepared to make the one final slash that would end the battle. "Now… where was I?"

Rocky uncoiled from below and, with a water-rending yell, his massive tail flashed through the water and hit Ferox full in the face. The blow sent a shockwave through the Rock Pool and stunned all who looked on. The force of the blow spattered teeth from Ferox's fractured jaw and caused blood to seep from his eyes.

"I... AM... SALMON!" roared Rocky in a voice that none had heard before. It was a voice of anguish and anger; it was a voice that released years of sadness and shame. "I... AM... SALMON!" he bellowed again. His face had become a mask of the purest, darkest, deepest rage. It was a look that shocked even the Hofsin, who looked on.

With another explosion of thunderous release, Rocky hurled himself at Ferox. Rocky's toothless jaws clamped hard on the loose flesh as he drove the thrashing Ferox ferociously upwards, until he crashed and collided with the ice. He pushed the squirming body hard against the frozen ceiling, which began to crack with the pressure. He pushed so hard that Ferox's head burst through the ice into the freezing cold air above. Ferox wriggled and screamed for all he was worth but, slowly and surely, Rocky pushed and heaved the hellish frame out and onto the ice. And there he stayed. The water froze back over again, leaving Ferox to thrash and flop around like a flounder. He drowned an agonising death in the freezing air.

The Rock Pool returned to silence and not a word was uttered as Rocky swam over to where Ferox's trout huddled. He eyed them steadily, his body still shaking from combat. He looked at them with loathing, yet when he spoke his voice had returned to its usual monotone.

"Now, I will tell you... Go away. Go away and never return to this place."

The trout were too scared to speak. Each in turn cowered in front of Rocky before darting away into the darkness, never to return. When they had gone, Rocky drifted downwards to rest beside Storlax, who lay motionless, save for the slow pounding of his gills. Blood streaked into the water from his wounds.

"You should not have done that, Rocky," Storlax coughed.

Rocky answered in his steady, slow voice. "Ferox is dead and his followers will not trouble us again. The nests are safe. He had to die."

Storlax heaved a great sigh. "Thank you. Thank you, Rocky. I didn't think that you would be able to fight."

"Nor did I," said Rocky, as he fanned soft streams of water across Storlax's wounds. He paused and then, almost in tears, added, "I could not let you, the one who saved me, I could not let you die. "

"You know, Ferox was right about one thing." There was a brief lightness to Storlax's voice.

"What's that?"

"Rocky isn't much of a name for a salmon, for that is what you are – a salmon. I am proud to call you that by name!"

Rocky smiled a shy slow smile. "Thank you, Storlax, but Rocky suits me fine."

'Rocky… come closer. I have to tell you something." Storlax's voice was frail as Rocky edged closer.

"What is it, my friend?" he asked.

"I can't see, Rocky. I can't see out of my eye… Ferox has blinded me."

"Oh, my poor friend," sighed Rocky.

"How can I lead the Hofsin back to the sea? What will I do?"

"I will guide you, Storlax. I will swim with you. Don't worry. Here, let me have a look." Rocky inspected the wound. "It's been badly scratched but it may heal, Storlax, it may heal."

Storlax slowly regained some strength into his tired body. "Help me get up and away from these rocks, I must talk to my Hofsin." Rocky helped and supported Storlax as he floated upwards. They were greeted by solemn, proud looks. They showed the deepest respect and admiration Hofsin can give.

"Come on, my brave Hofsin, we have..." Storlax started to address his clan in the way a king does after a major battle, but was interrupted by a warm jolly voice.

"Now what is all this commotion? How dare you disturb the peace and quiet of the river with your fighting, Solo?" Storlax recognised the voice and heard his old name. It brought a smile to his battered and weary face.

"And just look at you! What in the Deep's name have you been up to, Solo? And is that Rocky I see with you?"

Storlax looked sightlessly to where the voice had come from. "Nanny! My dear Nanny Charr!" His voice crackled with emotion. "Nanny Charr, you restore my spirits!"

The kindly looking fish swam forward to greet Storlax. She fussed over the King in a way that Salto had never seen before. "So many new scars, Solo! You really must be more careful. And what are doing up here at this time of year chasing Ferox? You should leave that to the young bloods. Rocky, you too should know better. I've got a good mind to slap both your fins!"

Storlax looked sheepishly at Nanny Charr and was not a little embarrassed to be treated as a young smolt in front of his brave Hofsin.

"Come on, Nanny Charr, we had best go to the Home Pool so that you can visit the nests. It will soon be time for us to leave for the sea."

"Well that's why I'm here. I've looked forward to this moment all summer. Come on, Rocky, you swim with me. You can tell me all that has happened on this Great Journey."

Rocky and Nanny Charr swam on. Salto positioned himself against Storlax's flank, which helped to level his body in the water.

"Who is Nanny Charr?" asked Salto as they slowly made their way back to the Home Pool. "There is something familiar about her but I don't know what it is. She has a scent of happiness about her."

Storlax smiled and replied, "Of course you know her! It's just that we salmon forget everything until we are smolts. Nanny Charr looked after you when you were in the nest. When we salmon leave the river, we leave our nests to her care and protection. She tends and cherishes our young, while we return to the sea to mend and feed."

"I see, but who is she? How do we know we can trust her?" Salto would have asked more questions but Storlax stopped him.

"Salto, Salto. Nanny Charr has been in the river for as long as any Hofsin can remember. She is the 'River Amma' – every river has one. And so long as the River Amma is here, then there will always be salmon in the river. She is every salmon's grandmother. She cares for and protects our eggs when we leave. Now you see a charming old charr, but as you grow older you will see a kind soul. It is this kind soul that is the very soul of the river – our river." Salto saw a small tear of happiness form in the corner of Storlax's wounded eye. "She is my Nanny Charr, and she alone calls me Solo!"

Storlax and Salto edged their way back to the Home Pool. Salto led the way down to the slacker water below the banks with Storlax's nose pressed firmly against the young Hofsin's tail. Try as he could, Salto found it impossible to avoid the rocks that lay in their path and he shuddered each time he heard Storlax thump into another boulder and groan.

"I'm sorry, Storlax."

"Don't worry, you're doing well. We must press on, we must press on..." said Storlax through his pain. "We can rest when we reach the Home Pool... the Home Pool..." He repeated the words; they gave him comfort.

In a while they rounded a long bend and Salto hesitated as he waited at the top of the shallow, streamy run that lay at the head of the pool. The thick ice had left the narrowest of passages for them to swim through. Storlax sensed the stiffening of the current and heard the fizz of rushing water. He sensed Salto's unease.

"Swim on, boy. Swim on! We are almost there," and with these words Storlax pushed Salto forwards, trying his best to mask his pain as he banged across the gravel river bed into the safety of the Home Pool.

There, waiting for him, was Nanny Charr. "Welcome home, Solo."

A smile of recognition and relief spread across Storlax's weary brow and his voice found strength. "Nanny Charr... I am home indeed!"

"I have found you a bed of the softest weed, Solo. There you can lay and mend until the thaw comes."

"I can't see, Nanny Charr," whispered Storlax.

"I know, I know," comforted the kindly old fish. "You must gain your strength, Solo. Your Hofsin need you to take them back to the sea."

"I'm blind. It's hopeless," sighed Storlax.

"Shush, now. Who knows what the future holds? Shush now, and follow me."

Storlax was too tired to speak any more. He did as he was told, nudging his head against the proffered tail of Nanny Charr. She took him to a deep cut at the side of the Home Pool and there she nudged silken fronds of weed around Storlax's wounded body. With soothing words, she sent the King to the edge of a winter's trance. With glazed eyes and a smile, he listened to her stories of the adventures of all the Storlax before him. These sagas reminded him that, mighty as he was, he was powerless before the Deep, that his whole life had been mapped and planned well before he was born in the Home Pool, all those years ago, and that this struggle was just a part of that plan. He would prove his greatness by leading his Hofsin back to the sea and safety. When Nanny Charr had finished her stories, Storlax sighed and, as his darkness deepened, began to enjoy the deepest, happiest winter's trance he had ever known.

Part 3

The Great Thaw

And so, the great thaw came.

A warm, wet wind blasted from the south west, bringing a torrential rain, which poured down onto the land for many days. The snow that had lain thick over the mountains and hills began to melt and the river, which had only a few days ago been frozen, now flowed in a powerful, forbidding torrent. Nanny Charr swam to the weed bed where Storlax lay. He was already alert.

"Is that you, Nanny Charr?" he asked expectantly.

"Yes, it's me. The thaw has started, Solo. You must leave before the waters rise too high." She paused and then added, "How do you feel?"

"Far stronger and I feel no pain now, but I still can't see. What can I do?"

"You must trust the Deep," Nanny Charr urged.

"But I can't see! I've been straining to grasp the slightest image, but there is nothing, nothing but the dark. What of my Hofsin? How have they fared?"

"They are all frightened, Storlax. If you could see them you would see the look of fear. The thaw has come quickly, the river is in torrent with huge lumps of ice adding to the crush of muddy water. Many are talking of staying until it goes."

"They can't stay. The flood will worsen and we will be flushed over the falls and crushed by ice and rock. They must have food. We must leave and I must lead them!" Storlax spoke as the King of old.

"Well, I can help you no more, Solo. It is your destiny to lead your Hofsin to the sea. You alone know what to do now," Nanny Charr said solemnly as she drifted to one side.

There was silence in the pool. Storlax breathed deeply. In his silent communion he willed to see the Deep with all his might. He pleaded for strength and guidance to lead his Hofsin over the Great Falls. His faith was rewarded by twisting beams which filled his mind. It was if a swirling beam spread from above and bathed the weed bed where Storlax lay. His eyes remained scarred and sightless but, behind them, his mind could picture the river that he and his ancestors had travelled for so many centuries. He could see the way ahead as if it were the brightest of summer's days. His eyes were blind, but his soul had become one with the river's spirit. He could see no fish or rock but knew the way ahead. He could sense the way to safety. Nothing could stop him now.

"I am ready." His voice was the voice of a king. "I am ready to lead my Hofsin to the sea! Now, Nanny Charr, call Rocky over to me. I am going to need his strength as never before."

Through the murky turmoil Rocky's silhouette appeared, but before he could speak Storlax addressed him: "The Power of the Deep is with me, Rocky. I will lead my Hofsin over the Great Falls one last time. I can picture the way ahead as if it were my first leap, but my body is weak. I will need you by my side."

"To the end, Storlax. To the end," Rocky murmured.

With their flanks touching, they floated upwards and could feel that the water had become warmer as it swirled powerfully away to the tail of the pool. "This is going to be a high flood indeed," whispered Storlax, as they approached the clan.

Storlax gazed sightlessly around him as he chided the cowering Hofsin. "Well, what a pitiful clan. We have the Great Falls to plunge and beyond is the sea. This is why we are Hofsin. This is our moment. We are the finest leapers of all the salmon. How can you cower here when our greatest challenge lies ahead?" He paused and glowered at them. "Are you Hofsin?" his voice boomed. "Well, answer me! Are you Hofsin?"

"WE ARE HOFSIN!" came the joyous reply from voices that had found new courage.

He exhaled heavily. "It is time to go. You must take great care on the journey downstream. The river is high, the current is strong and we are weak. Keep to the bank and keep your heads to the current. Do not point downstream, save in the slack water, or you will be washed away and drowned! When we reach the Falls, let us prove our worth and take them like true Hofsin!" There were cheers from one and all as Storlax continued, "We will try to keep together, but the river is in a treacherous state. If we are divided we will meet again under the Shadowgate. There we can tell our tales of glory!"

Turning to Rocky, he whispered, "Swim close, brother, swim close."

Rocky came to a halt. "Say that again," he said quietly.

Storlax smiled and said deeply, "Brother... *my* brother!"

"I like that name," mused Rocky.

"Well, 'Brother' it is then."

Nanny Charr swam over to Storlax. "Well, Solo, I will not see you again for a long while but if it is meant, then we will meet again."

Storlax tried to speak but for once he was speechless.

" Shh... You have done well, my King. Travel in the knowledge that you have, indeed, been a great king. The Hofsin will be proud of you and hold you forever in their hearts. Now, off you go... off you go. And as for you, Rocky, you know what you must do. You carry a heavy burden." Rocky nodded silently and swallowed his sadness.

Storlax turned and swam away with tears in his sightless eyes. This was the first time Nanny Charr had called him King. He would not see her again in this life.

"Now come on, Brother. We have an adventure ahead of us!" he shouted through his emotion.

Storlax and Rocky slipped backwards with the current and disappeared out of sight. Soon a mighty bellow could be heard as the two giant fish turned downstream and hurled themselves over the lip of the Great Falls. Soon all would follow.

Salto and Una huddled together with Nanny Charr. "Now off you go, you two. I'll look after your nest and if the Deep is willing, I will see you again. Safe journey!"

With these words, Salto and Una edged into the current, and in seconds they were carried out of sight. They stayed together for as long as they could but, as they approached the Great Falls, the current swirled and rolled around them, forcing them to point downstream towards the perilous plunge over the ledge.

"Don't worry, Una, I am behind you!" Salto shouted.

Over the Falls

Eagle soared over the Great Falls. He circled in the cloud that hung over the gorge and eyed the raging torrent with alarm for, below him, he saw the greatest flood that he had witnessed in all his many years. From time to time, he could see black shapes propelled over the lip of the pool; they shot into the air before tumbling into the bubbling water below. These shapes were Hofsin who had no option but to yield their fate to the hands of the Deep. He saw, too, white boulders of ice that drifted towards the edge before being lost to the thunderous spray that swirled like steam over the Great Falls. He circled for a while in the turbulent air, watching the Hofsin as they plunged into the abyss. Some crashed onto the rocks and were killed, most swam away to safety, but all were powerless against the implacable force of Nature. Eagle flapped a lazy wing as he turned to fly back to shelter in the mouth of a cave – he had witnessed enough.

There, he perched with Raven and Snowy Owl. They squatted together in sombre discussion. Eagle comforted his friends that behind this, the bleakest of times, was spring, waiting to unveil herself. With her would come the promise of a new year. But Snowy Owl knew the thoughts behind Eagle's words; he knew that Eagle feared for Storlax and for the Prince of the Hofsin. Snowy Owl plumped up his white, downy feathers and sighed the way he and his ancestors have sighed, since anyone can remember, when a Fur, Fin or Feather king was in mortal danger. Raven and Eagle could just hear the whispered word "*S-t-o-r-l-a-x*" buried in the midst of the sigh. They looked at one another and then ambled and rolled, in their respective ways, to the ledge at the front of the cave, gazing to where the mist hung over the Great Falls in the distance. Snowy Owl remained in the gloom where his eyes felt more comfortable. He was no friend of the daylight, for in its glare he could see but little; he needed all of his mystic powers to see through the wildness of the river to the valiant Hofsin who struggled below its surface.

———

Storlax landed in the deepest part of the pool. Ice and spume covered the surface and swirled in all directions. Storlax was not afraid though. He enjoyed the press of water and the explosion of bubbles on his battered body, he cared not whether he was upside down or facing the wrong way; he was alive at the head of his Hofsin. The Power of the Deep was with him. It called him to the sea. He could see the way ahead through the wildest of currents.

"Follow me!" his voice boomed as he was hit by the shockwave of Rocky's body, crashing down into the water beside him. "Swim with me, Brother!"

Rocky tried to speak but was too winded by the fall.

"Have you ever seen anything like this?" Storlax marvelled at Nature's forces.

"We must swim away from here," gasped Rocky.

Storlax ignored him. The King was held spellbound. He felt untouchable, he felt that nothing could or would harm him. "I've never seen it like this before – so majestic, so mighty, so powerful!" shouted Storlax.

"This day will go down in our history. And you are with me, Brother. Your name will be spoken of with mine for years to come!"

Rocky feared for his friend, he seemed half-crazed. "Storlax, here, come with me. Over here."

"It's magnificent!" boomed Storlax.

"Follow me." Rocky's words were now a gentle command.

Reluctantly, Storlax followed Rocky out of the cauldron, his whole body trembling with excitement. The King ranted and raved about the splendour of it all, as lumps of ice and Hofsin plunged all around him. Storlax laughed and roared as Rocky coaxed him to safety. He let the current push them to the side of the river and, there, Rocky found a long shallow depression in front of a boulder, where they could rest. He swam forward to enter it but was stopped by the smallest of voices, which he could just hear above the hubbub of the pool.

"Don't come any further!" the voice commanded.

"What?" said Storlax. "Who's that?"

"Don't come into our lie," the voice added nervously. "I'm warning you…"

Rocky smiled, but it was Storlax who spoke. "Do you know who I am?" The King's voice was almost lighthearted.

"No, but I must do my duty, I must protect these small fry. They are the Hofsin's future!"

"Come forward and let me see you, 'Guardian of our future'," Storlax said as the young smolt finned himself nervously towards him. "And what is your name?"

"My name is Brynjar, Brynjar of the Hofsin, and these fry here are in my charge. Don't come any further."

Rocky peered behind Brynjar and there, in a quivering, huddled mass, were the small fry that he had charged the young smolt to look after.

"Brynjar, it's me, Rocky. Are you all right?" The smolt peered at Rocky with tired eyes through the murky water and smiled with relief when he realised that his task would soon be over. "Have these small fry behaved themselves?" Rocky asked.

"Oh well, they've been pretty good, really," said Brynjar, in a voice that suggested the opposite. The smolt was gaunt and spare from weeks of minding his charges. He should have been out at sea feeding and growing into a young Hofsin. Rocky was proud of him.

"Well, you tell them that they are about to share their home with Storlax, King of the Hofsin."

Rocky turned to talk to Storlax and saw that the King had once again become weak. He had lost the wildness in his face and had become muddled. Rocky whispered into his ear. "You must thank young Brynjar here for all that he has done while we have been upstream. He is a fine young smolt."

"Yes, quite so, quite so," said Storlax as he finned closer to the smolt. And, after Storlax had thanked Brynjar and gazed appreciatively in the direction of the small fry, Rocky led the King to the most sheltered part of the hollow. "Rest here," Rocky comforted. "Rest here, Storlax. I must find Salto. We need him to be with us now." He turned to Brynjar and said, "Now you have the most solemn duty; you and your fry must guard your King while I am away."

The tiredness fell away from Brynjar as he filled with pride and assembled his fry around Storlax in the sheltered trench.

———

Una made her leap. She was hurled, nose over tail, into the foaming cauldron at the bottom of the Falls. There she plunged to the depths of the pool. She had hoped to find shelter to rest for a while and wait for Salto, but the river had no such plans for her; she was swept away and down into the gorge beyond. She rolled over and over in the water. It was as if she was being propelled by a great hurtling whirlpool. Her head crashed against a rock, she became dazed and confused. Her excitement turned to fear; she could not breathe.

"Salto... Salto!" she mouthed, but no noise came from her. She was too dazed to speak. She felt life drifting away from her. She could feel her body giving up the struggle, and then Rocky appeared through the swirling current. She could see his soft smile veiled in the torrent.

"Hold on Una... Hold on, Una..." his voice coaxed. "Rest on me... you are safe now." His body swam sideways into her to stop her drifting further downstream. She leant against him, panting heavily. He curved his body inwards to cradle her. They came to rest against a large block of rock.

"Where is Salto? Is he with us?" she gasped.

"I haven't seen him yet," said Rocky. "I must get you to safety. The water is too wild here."

"No, I want to wait for him. He was just behind me. I'm staying here," demanded Una. She gave Rocky a look that told him it was pointless to argue. He saw blood trailing from the knock on her head. She had been hurt but he knew, too, that nothing would make her leave. She would wait for Salto.

"Well, you tuck in behind me. You can shelter from the current there and we can wait for young Salto together."

Una dropped behind Rocky and nuzzled her head against his tail. There she was protected from the worst of the current.

Finally came Salto. He ignored Storlax's advice and decided instead to meet the challenge of the Falls head on. He swam into the middle of the Home Pool's current and, thrashing his tail with all the strength that he could muster, shot downstream in a blur of spray. Then, in the thunderous turmoil of rushing water, he hurled himself over the precipice. Floating in the air, he could see the river below him; he could feel the whistling of the wind in his gills; his eyes stung. He was alive with excitement – he throbbed with adventure. For a fleeting moment he was an eagle on the wing. "Yeeehaaaah!" he yelled to the world, as he plummeted headlong towards the seething, foaming effervescence below.

Below him, a jagged boulder of ice broke free from the Block of Destiny and was thrown by the current across his path. Although Salto twisted and swerved in the air, he hit the solid lump with a glancing blow that sent him reeling sideways and crashing down onto the rocks below. He had been knocked clear of the river. Salto, Prince of the Hofsin, floundered on the land. He lay lifelessly on a giant rock beside the torrent; nearby were the bodies of other Hofsin who had also been defeated by the Great Falls.

The Black Eyes

Rocky and Una peered through the water, searching for Salto. They asked each Hofsin that passed whether they had seen him, but none had. Rocky turned to Una; he sighed as he saw her searching the water in desperation.

"Una, we must go now."

"No," was her simple reply.

"Una," Rocky paused and sighed. "Una, something must have happened to Salto. We would have seen him by now."

"He's here somewhere. I can feel him near me. He's here, Rocky, I know it."

"Una, we have to get Storlax back to the sea. Maybe Salto was washed downstream. He could be waiting for us under the Shadowgate."

"He's here, I tell you. Talk as much as you want, but I'm not leaving." Una stared defiantly at Rocky, who smiled sadly at her in reply.

"Well, I can't force you. I'll go and gather up Storlax and let's hope that we all meet at the Shadowgate." He nuzzled his head against hers. "Don't stay too long, Una. The river will only get worse."

"I'll bring him to the sea. Don't you worry!" said Una.

Rocky sighed as he drifted into the current and then swam hard across the press of water to the boulder where he had left Storlax. He returned to find the King telling Brynjar and the small fry adventures from his past. They listened in wonder.

"There's nothing more frightening than a seal in hot pursuit. See this?" Storlax showed them the three parallel scars on his flank. His young audience gasped. "A seal did that to me. Now, there's only one way to escape a seal, and that is to swim fast and deep – fast and deep! You see, the seal can't swim as deep as we can. If he does, his eyes pop out!" The small fry giggled and writhed as their King told them this. "So remember, fast and deep and don't look back. If you let him chase you into the shallows, you'll get one of these…" he peered darkly at them, "…or worse still, you'll get gobbled up alive!" Storlax laughed a deep, hearty, sinister laugh. "Like this!" He opened his huge mouth and pretended to swallow a whole salmon.

The small fry pleaded with Storlax to tell them another story but the King sensed Rocky's return.

"What news, Rocky? Where's Salto?"

"No one has seen him."

"Oh no, not the Prince. It can't be! Maybe he's at the Shadowgate." But Storlax's voice held little hope.

"Perhaps. Una is going to wait here. But we must go, Storlax. You need the sea. We must get as many Hofsin to sea as we can; they must eat," Rocky said.

"Yes, you are right, but I fear for Salto." Storlax sighed heavily and then, looking at Brynjar, he said solemnly, "And as for you, my fine young smolt, do you think that you can lead your shoal downstream with us to safer water?"

"Yes, sir!" replied the smolt.

"Follow us then, follow us."

Rocky sidled up to Storlax and let the King lean against him as they started to pick their way downstream in the treacherous swirls and boils of the flooded river. They made slow and laboured progress; each boulder, trench and eddy held Hofsin. Tired and weary from their plunge, they swam to join their King. The shoal grew as it swam in silence downstream. None spoke of their dread fear, that Salto, Prince of the Hofsin, had been lost to the might of the Great Falls.

———

Years of erosion had worn the boulder's once jagged surface to a smooth depression, like a dish, in which Salto now lay slumped. A shallow pool had formed at the bottom, fed by spray from the Great Falls; it fell like heavy mist onto the rock, making it sleek and slippery, but it also gave Salto just sufficient moisture to breath. He looked in alarm at his surroundings and quickly realised that there was no escape. He cursed himself for his stupidity in ignoring Storlax's advice and, beyond his anger, he could sense Una in the river below, waiting for him.

His eyes stung from the air and he held his head so that drips of water would run across them, easing the pain and helping him to see. With each drip he was able to look out for a while and on the fifth occasion, when his eyes had become accustomed to the air, he saw in the distance two small eyes looking back at him – two black, pitiless beads. He felt fear well up inside him. These were the two eyes that he had glimpsed on the

Block of Destiny before the winter, and now they were staring icily at him. He was helpless.

Salto squirmed and writhed on the slippery rock but it was hopeless. He groaned silently in his despair and his gills opened and closed strenuously as they tried to suck as much moisture from the air as they could. More spray washed over his eyes and his despair turned to panic when he saw the sharp teeth beneath the black eyes, chewing on the flesh of a Hofsin. Salto mustered all the strength he could find and, ignoring the pain, thrashed his tail against the rock. His body arched as he slipped upwards to the lip of the bowl. His head peered over the rim and below he could make out the river. He slapped again and edged further forward, but a slew of spray cascaded down upon him, causing him to slither back to the bottom of the bowl.

He looked upwards and cried out aloud, for now, there on the rim eyeing him coldly, was Mink.

"We don't want to lose you, do we?" Mink whispered darkly.

Salto looked defiantly at Mink but his heart trembled and shook with the purest fear.

"A fine young Hofsin… I'll take you to my hole… nice young flesh… rich pickings until the spring…"

Salto whimpered and moaned as he tried to slither away.

"We can't let you slip away, young Hofsin. One bite on that neck of yours, and you're mine!" Mink raised herself on her hind legs and her fur pressed sleek and wet against her slender body. She coiled backward, the claws on her front paws bared and ready to pounce. Salto braced himself for the worst but, instead of feeling sharp teeth on his neck, he heard the whistling of wind through wings, and the sound of claws on rock. He peered upwards and there sat Raven, his purple-black feathers spread wide and his eyes, dark as time itself, glaring at Mink. Raven folded his wings and adjusted his perch but never let his gaze wander from the crouched rodent in front of him.

"Go away, Raven, I found him first. He's mine to eat," Mink said, as she settled down on all fours.

Raven answered by ruffling the water from his wings.

"Get out of my way, you old crow! Go! There's plenty there for everyone," hissed Mink.

Raven shook his head and slid down the rock to where Salto lay, his claws struggling to hold the slippery surface. He squatted beside Salto and unfurled his wings to their full extent, then curled them forwards to cover and protect the Hofsin's body. Raven's head stood defiantly erect above his feathered shield.

"Get out my way! I'm not scared of you, Raven. Your beak holds no fear for me. You are as helpless as that Hofsin against my teeth and claws." Mink waved a clawed paw as she spoke.

Raven pulled his robe of wings even closer to Salto and braced himself for the onslaught. Still he did not speak.

Mink was hissing with outrage. She prowled in tight circles, then raised herself onto her hind legs and pulled her mouth back into a vicious, menacing snarl. "If you want to save yourself, fly now, Raven!"

Through the mist came a swirling, whistling and whooshing and down swooped Eagle. His huge wingspan darkened the sky for an instant and then, like wind through the trees, he was gone as quickly as he had come. Gone too was Mink, who had been grasped in Eagle's talons.

Eagle beat his wings and flew upwards, over the Great Falls and on for some distance into the mountains. He held Mink lightly, ignoring her hissing and spitting as he let an updraft carry them inland. Soon he dipped his wings and glided slowly downwards to earth. There, he placed her on a mossy bank before settling nearby.

"Have you ever flown before?" Eagle laughed as he asked the question, but Mink was in no mood for laughter. She hissed and spat as she prowled in a circle around him.

"How dare you do that to me!"

"Raven stopped you killing the one who is destined to lead the Hofsin. He is the next Storlax. Without a leader the salmon will fail and if that happens there will be none to eat in years to come. Now do you understand? If you killed that salmon, there would be none for your children to feed on. You must see the wisdom in this."

"I don't need your wisdom. I can only do what I know is best for me. Next year is another year; I have to survive this one first. If there are no salmon I'll feed on something else. Now get out of my way!"

"Mink, Mink, I urge to think about these things. All of us, Fur, Fin and Feather, who were here before the Shadows came to this land, lived in abundance. We killed and fed in the way that we do but there was balance, moderation. The Shadows arrived and changed things forever. That is why we have the Parliament of the Animals. The Shadows brought you, too, and when your ancestors escaped into the wild you were welcomed into the parliament. Despite our pleas you have ignored our requests to moderate. 'Take from one nest, not all. Take one fish, not all.' How often were you told that? It can't go on Mink. It can't go on!"

"It's the way we are, Eagle, and you have no option but to respect this. It is our nature. We were brought here in cages, we escaped and we survived as best we could. We have since been poisoned, trapped, hunted and skinned by the Shadows. We survive by our wits and our cunning. We know no other way and it is not for you to stop us. We don't need you or your parliament."

Eagle shook his head sadly and spread his wings ready to fly. "I had hoped that you would see reason." He turned to face the wind, made two hops forward and then sprang upwards, beating hard with his wings. Slowly he rose from the ground.

"You can't leave me here!" Mink shouted. But Eagle was deaf to her pleading. In her frustration and anger she screamed, "I'll never forgive you for this, Eagle. I know where you nest. I'll have your eggs come the spring. You'll regret this. I swear you'll regret this!"

Eagle sighed deeply as he soared upwards in the warm moist air. He knew that what Mink had said was right, that in protecting the Hofsin Prince he had upset the balance of nature. There would be a price to pay in the future. He cursed the Shadows as never before and, with a heavy heart, he returned to the cave to join Snowy Owl.

To the Sea

Raven unfolded his wings. Salto lay with his gills pumping frantically for water, his heart beating faster than ever. He was dizzy with shock and fear. He moaned as Raven tried to push him up the slope with the side of his beak, but the rock was too slippery for his claws to grip and Salto was too heavy. Raven slipped, slithered and pushed, but it was no good – the Hofsin was too much for him. Raven heard a mighty cracking and creaking distinct above the roar of the Falls. He looked up and was terrified to see a huge slab of ice working its way over the lip of the Falls. For a few moments it hung perilously above them and then, with a mighty explosion, it broke free and hurtled down towards them. Raven squawked in alarm and threw his wings over Salto once more, to protect him. He ducked his head, bracing himself for the impact, but none came. The vast slab whistled past them, splintering on the rim of the bowl before crashing into the water below. Raven raised his head in relief, only to see the deluge that had been let loose by the ice cascade and tumble down onto them. Raven and Salto were sluiced sideways by the press of water and flushed out over the edge and down into the river below. Salto slipped elegantly into the river, while Raven was dumped unceremoniously into the foaming torrent and swept away, his outstretched wings keeping him afloat. Gradually he flapped and scrambled to the shore where, squawking with indignation, he shook himself on the bank. He remained staring at the river, willing the Hofsin a safe journey to the sea. Then, bending his black spindly legs, he sprung himself upwards and pounded the air with his wings. He flew up and over the Great Falls, back to the cave and his companions. There were stories to be told and shared. Raven knew that the episode with Mink had put something in motion that would not rest easily. There was much talking and thinking to be done before the spring came.

Salto sucked deep draughts of water through his gills as he let the current take him downstream. In his confusion he heard a voice.

"Salto?... oh Salto!... I knew you were alive. I knew it!"

Una nudged and pushed Salto downstream until she found a sheltered corner where they could rest.

"You will not *believe* what has just happened to me," said the dazed Salto.

"Sshh... sshh... all in good time. You must rest," Una said to her friend, who was more dead than alive.

Rocky watched as Storlax rested in a back eddy downstream of the Shadowgate, where Brynjar and the small fry were playing. The sound of their laughter helped the King forget his wounds. Some of the elders had approached Storlax and asked who would lead them if Salto had been taken by the Great Falls. Storlax had shooed them away angrily.

"Salto is alive. And he will stay alive until I, Storlax, say he is dead, and not before. We will wait here until he comes. Now leave me to the young!"

The elders were unhappy with this reply. They believed that Salto was lost and, moreover, they were hungry and wanted to get to the sea and as far from the river as possible. The sandbar held no fears at this time of year; the gulls were feeding at sea and with the mighty flood, the salmon would be washed out into the estuary and food in no time. At first in pairs, and then in larger groups, they left, until only Storlax and Rocky remained with the little ones. Rocky finned slowly over to where Storlax lay. He was about to tell him that they were alone when Storlax asked, "Have they all gone?"

"Yes, we're the last."

"You mustn't fret, my Brother. I understand why. It's the right thing for them to do. They are all famished. You must be hungry, too."

"I am." Rocky paused and then added quietly, "It's time for the sea, Storlax. We must go…"

"He's not dead, you know. I know Salto is not dead," Storlax said.

"It's been too long, Storlax. We would have heard news by now." And then Rocky said in the kindest of voices, "You have to prepare yourself, my friend."

"He is still alive and so am I. I am still Storlax, King of the Hofsin. Blind and old I might be, but I must get strong again." He sucked water through his gills. "Do you know, I can almost smell the sea. If we leave now, by nightfall we'll be feeding."

Rocky was pleased that they would be leaving the river and he watched as Storlax called Brynjar and the small fry to him.

"Now then," Storlax said solemnly. "It is time for us to leave the river. Brynjar is going to swim with me. You have learnt much from him this winter and now it is time for you to fend for yourselves. You'll be safe here as long as you do as you have been told."

Several small fry rushed to Brynjar and pleaded with him not to go. "What's that I hear? Tears?" asked Storlax. "No, no, we are Hofsin. We don't cry when we say goodbye! We smile, happy in the knowledge of our friendship, in the trust of our fellowship and of good times to come. No tears here, now. No tears for Hofsin."

These were the same words that Storlax had been told by his King all those years ago and, try as he might, he found it hard not to mask his sadness. His voice croaked as he said, "The quicker we go, the sooner we'll be back," and a lumpy smile formed across his battle-scarred face as he turned to Rocky and said, " To the sea. To the sea!"

Rocky turned to swim with Storlax downstream in the easing current and Brynjar paddled beside them.

Storlax and Rocky found themselves once again in the estuary. The river and the Shadows were now behind them. They tasted the brackish water and felt the gentle ebb of the tide. Rocky looked at Storlax as he tried to chase the minnows that wallowed in front of his nose. But it was hopeless; Storlax could not feed himself. Rocky caught a few and blew them into the King's waiting mouth. Storlax smiled gratefully, but he realised that his blindness meant that he would never feed himself again. Their wasted stomachs soon filled and the meagre meal gave the King new heart. They drifted happily as the tide carried them away from the river.

"Hello, my fine friends!" said a voice that brought a smile to Rocky's face.

"Red Belly?" said Rocky.

"The very same. And how are you, Rocky? Is that not the mighty Storlax I see behind you?"

"Hello, Red Belly," said Storlax in his most kingly way. "How's life been treating you?"

"Oh, you know, the same old thing. Me and my rock, we don't have much to offer the world," said Red Belly with his usual happy smile. "I haven't seen so many of your Hofsin come past this year."

"No, it has not been an easy year for us. The flood was very high," Storlax said gravely. "We've lost many good friends." Rocky nodded.

"Well, that's what happens in this watery world of ours. It's hard to make any sense out of anything. I've given up trying." Red Belly thought for a while and then said, "You can't be much longer for this life yourself, Storlax. You look dreadful!"

"Well, thank you, Red Belly. I'll bear it in mind!" replied Storlax grumpily.

"No offence meant, but I've seen you and your Hofsin come and go for many years now. Isn't it about time you made a new Storlax?"

Storlax smiled proudly, "We will have a fine new Storlax. His name is Salto."

Red Belly smiled a beaming smile, remembering his meeting with the young Hofsin all those moons ago. "Well, you couldn't make a better choice, if I might say so. He's strong and brave, but he's kind and sensitive, too. I like that in a salmon!"

"Just so, just so," chuckled Storlax. He then turned to Rocky and said "My brother, I've been thinking. Why don't you stay here with your old friend Red Belly. You would probably like some brighter company. This estuary water is not what I need. I need the open sea. Young Brynjar here can lead me and there's much for him to learn. Besides, he's better at catching minnows than you!"

"No Storlax. I stay with you until the end."

"Well, I'd rather you stay here and wait for Salto."

Rocky tried to speak, but Storlax stopped him. "Please, my brother, don't make this harder than it is already. Let's part with a smile and be grateful for our friendship." Rocky knew it was pointless to argue with Storlax. He smiled bravely. "And Red Belly!" Storlax boomed, as of old. "You look after my brother here. Make sure he feeds well and tells you the tales of this, the greatest of all the Great Journeys."

"I'll do that, don't you worry. And farewell to you, Storlax. I wish I'd got to know you better. Journey well, wherever it is you're going," said Red Belly, not sure whether he was happy or sad, but smiling anyway.

"Brynjar. Come here, boy!" commanded Storlax. "Swim just here, in front of my nose, let me feel your ripples across my brow, and I'll follow you. Swim as you've never swum before, follow the sun until it sets and beyond."

And then, with a look that said more than words could ever say, he gazed at Rocky. It was a look that banished all sadness from the friend who had become his brother. In that look, they both recognised that they were fortunate indeed to have known one another, and that they would meet again in the Deep. They parted in unspoken happiness.

And so, on the dregs of the tide, Storlax followed Brynjar out to sea. The King did not look back.

Journey's End

Una gazed at Salto as he twitched and moaned lightly in his rest.

They had lain together for some time while Salto had told her of his adventure with Mink and how Raven and Eagle had come to save him. He had laughed when he told her that at first, when Raven covered him with his wings, he thought that the bird was going to eat him – and, when he saw the slab of ice tumbling down on top of them, that he would die for a fourth time that day. He had yawned and finally slipped into a deep rest, happy in the knowledge that Una was beside him.

"Salto… Salto…" whispered Una. "It's time to go. We must find Storlax. He'll be so worried."

"Mmh?" Salto stirred gently and winced as he stretched his bruised and battered body.

"The river is still rising, Salto. We must get going. We must leave now."

It took a few more moments before Salto was fully alert. He smiled gratefully at Una. "Thank you for waiting for me. I wouldn't have made it without you."

"Oh, you'd have been all right; it seems you're destined to survive," said Una modestly.

"No, you saved me, Una. You waited when everyone else had gone." Salto stretched again and then, feeling newly alive, said, "Come on, Una, I'll race you to the Shadowgate!"

And so they swam the flooding river. They tried to keep to the bank where the water flowed more gently but from time to time, when they swerved to avoid boulders, they were swept out into the main current. There, they shouted with glee at the excitement of it all. Soon the Shadowgate loomed in front of them and they slowed down, anxious to meet their fellow Hofsin.

"They've gone!" Salto was crestfallen. "They've left us. Storlax must think I'm dead. Come on, Una, we must find them; we must go to the estuary!" They swam on even harder, ignoring their hunger and pain.

They swam over the sandbar and into the estuary. There, they halted for a while, relishing the familiar smells of the sea. Comforted by the depth of water below they grazed on minnows, their first food since they had entered the river.

"You know, it all seems like a dream," Salto said, as he swallowed a particularly large mouthful.

"Well, I'm not sad to see the back of the river. It has sad memories."

"Yes, I know, but what stories we have to tell, what stories…" Salto was bursting to tell someone – anyone – of what had happened.

"Come on Salto, eat your fill and then we must press on."

They swam onwards until they heard voices and laughter in the distance. "I know who that will be. Come and meet a friend of mine," said Salto, as he led Una to Red Belly's rock.

"Good day!"

"Salto!" Rocky was overjoyed to see them.

"None other. Una, meet my dear friend, Red Belly. I've told you all about him."

"Well done, Una. Well done. You've brought him back to us!" Rocky's voice was full of joy.

"Have we got stories to tell you! You won't believe what happened…" Salto started, but Rocky interrupted.

"There is no time, Salto, not now. Storlax is very frail. He has swum on with Brynjar. He *must* know that you are alive. You will have to tell me your stories later."

"Oh dear, I'm sorry, Red Belly. I would have liked to have stayed and talked."

Red Belly smiled his cracked smile. "Oh, don't you worry about that, come and tell me next time you pass. But I have some advice."

"What is it?" Salto was curious.

"Well, you remember the little trick I showed you?"

Salto laughed and nodded as he thought of Red Belly exploding in bubbles away from him.

"Well, I'd forget it if I were you," continued Red Belly, "pretend it never happened, you know."

"Why?" asked Salto. "It was very funny."

"Yes, it is, but in my humble opinion…" he drew closer and whispered, "farting is not very kingly!"

"NO… IT'S… NOT!" Rocky said in agreement.

Salto smiled at Red Belly and said, "We must go, my friend, while the tide has some strength left in it. The Deep willing, I will see you again." He exchanged warm smiles with Rocky. They both knew that they would meet again.

Salto and Una swam together out of the estuary and soon they felt the swell of the ocean and the pull of the current on their bodies. The river and its dangers were behind them; ahead was the boundless ocean and below them the Deep. They swam fast and sure towards the dipping sun.

Salto shivered as they swam near the Nets of the Dead. He thought he could hear their siren voices saying, "Come to me. Please come to me?" He swam on in silent determination. His one thought was to find Storlax; he had become heedless of anything else.

Soon, in the distance, he could make out the noble silhouette of his mighty King, led by the nimble shadow of Brynjar. Una let Salto swim ahead. When he was close enough to be heard, he opened his mouth to speak, but hesitated. His whole body shook with emotion. All the excitement, danger and fear of the last few days welled up inside him. The only word he could say was. "Storlax…"

The King heard his name and stopped swimming. He drew a deep breath through his gills and sighed a deep sigh of contentment.

"So, you are here, young Salto of the Hofsin." Storlax sighed again and then, sensing another fish, asked, "Is that Una you have with you?"

""Yes, it is. She rescued me from the river. I have much to tell you…"

"And I you, my Prince." And then, in the most solemn of voices he said, "Una, thank you. This old King thanks you with all of his heart. You have done a great service to the Hofsin."

Without a word Una swam and signalled for Brynjar to follow her. Salto was about to tell her to stay with them, but she gestured that they would go to find the main shoal of Hofsin. Storlax and Salto swam on together.

The sinking sun shone down onto the rippled surface, causing the light to dance and play upon the waves. It cast bright beams down below, to where Storlax and Salto swam. It was as if the sun itself was welcoming the return of these two great fish to the ocean.

"I always knew you were alive, Salto. I always believed that," said Storlax. "This is your destiny."

"It feels good to be alive. I grow stronger with every wave of my tail," said Salto, as he swam ahead to chase a small shoal of capelin that glistened in the faltering light. He ate greedily. "These are so good!" He tried to feed some to Storlax, but the King had no appetite for them.

"So, tell me the story of what happened at the Great Falls. I must know. Tell me everything, don't miss out a thing," Storlax commanded.

As darkness fell, they swam together, further out to sea. Salto told Storlax the tale of Mink, Raven and Eagle at the Great Falls. He was shy at first but then, with words of encouragement, Salto told the story in its entirety. Storlax listened in deep contemplation, nodding and gasping as the tale unfolded. When it came to the end Storlax drew a deep, satisifed breath and said, "This is a marvellous tale. You cannot begin to understand how much this means to me. Your rescue by Raven and Eagle is a sign that your destiny and theirs are now linked together in a way that no other Hofsin's has ever been before. But their intervention also means that your fate will be tied with Mink's. You have not seen the last of her."

Salto listened quietly as he tried to understand.

"Well, all that's in the future…" said Storlax, "…in the future."

"We must both feed," said Salto, as he swam on ahead. "I'm sure that once you've had a rest and fed your fill you will feel much better, Storlax. Your fin will heal and, who knows, in time your eye may heal, then you'll be able to lead us all on one more Great Journey. What do you say?"

There was no reply. Salto turned to see that Storlax had fallen behind him and was slowly sinking into the darker, colder depths.

"No, Storlax, please, not now…"

Salto rushed to Storlax's side and saw the life ebbing away from him. He swam under his King and tried to nudge him forwards, to push him up and onwards.

"Please, Storlax, don't leave me, not now. Please don't leave me alone," pleaded Salto.

"My time is over, Salto, and yours is just beginning. You mustn't fear. You will be a fine Storlax. I am proud to call you by that name, Storlax!"

"Please no! Don't go! You can't leave me now. There is so much I need to know, I am not capable of leading the clan. I need you to be with me."

Salto nudged and pushed, but the weight was too much and they sank deeper.

"I will always be with you. You will carry me in your heart as I will carry you in mine. You will make a fine king and you will never be alone. Snowy Owl has seen your future and there are many adventures ahead. He foretells that you will be a great leader." A serene gleam flickered in the old King's eyes. He was at peace with himself. "I am tired now. I must go…"

"Please don't leave me!" Salto felt a deep and bitter loneliness well up inside him.

"You must let him go, Salto. It is *his* time."

Salto turned to see Una swimming beside him. Her face was strong and shone with a comforting smile. "It is his time. We must let him go. And it is your time too, Storlax of the Hofsin."

"Oh, Una…!"

"It's all right. There is nothing to fear. See how happy he is. Let us say our farewells together."

Salto and Una floated together and watched as the Deep received Storlax in its kind embrace. They watched as his huge frame sank deeper and deeper, following his journey until he was the smallest speck in the blue depths. And then, just as he was about to disappear entirely, there was a bright flash of light that shone for a second, like the last star of the night, before flickering and faltering to nothing.

The light shone brightly in Salto's eyes, flooding through every sinew of his body and filling his heart with courage and strength. Storlax was ready to lead his clan.

He turned to swim upwards and there, massed in front of him, were all the Hofsin who had made the Great Journey. As far as the eye could see, their silvery flanks glistened and gleamed. Salto recognised Brynjar's cheery smile amongst the serious faces; all had come to greet their new King, Storlax. They bowed their heads in the deepest respect.

"Swim with me, Una. Swim by my side," he said. "We have a way to go before we reach our journey's end."